SHERLOCK ACADEMY

The Holmes Brigade

F.C. Shaw

Other Books by F.C. Shaw

Sherlock Academy
Sherlock Academy: Watson's Case
The Magical Flight of Dodie Rue

SHERLOCK ACADEMY
THE HOLMES BRIGADE

Future House Publishing

Text © 2016 F.C. Shaw
Interior illustrations © 2016 Jeff Harvey and Tyler Stott
Cover illustration © 2016 Future House Publishing

This book is a work of fiction. Names, characters, places, and incidents are either the product of the author's imagination or are used fictitiously. Any resemblance to actual persons, living or dead, or to actual events or locales is entirely coincidental.

ISBN: 978-1-944452-20-9 (paperback)
ISBN: 978-1-944452-21-6 (epub)
ISBN: 978-1-944452-23-0 (mobipocket)
ISBN: 978-1-944452-22-3 (pdf)

Cover illustration by Tyler Stott
Developmental editing by Helena Steinacker
Substantive editing by Emma Hoggan
Copy editing by Jenna Parmley
Interior design by Michelle Lippold

To Westly and William,
Be courageous to follow your dreams
and be yourselves

221 Baker St.
London NW1

SA

Mr. Rollin E. Wilson
22 Primrose Lane
London NE2

At this joyous time of year
We wish you loads of Christmas cheer.

Happy Holidays from the staff at
Sherlock Academy of Fine Sleuths

Boxing Day

The Christmas card had come by post a few days before Christmas.

It made Rollie feel homesick. Not for home—he had been home on Christmas vacation for a week now. No, it made him homesick for school. He was schoolsick. And he still had three more weeks of vacation.

"Rollie! Lunch!" his mother called from downstairs.

Rollin E. Wilson set the Christmas card back on his desk. He plodded down the twelve steps from his watchtower-like bedroom to the second floor. From there, he hurried downstairs. He found his family gathered around the dining table. Chicken noodle soup, biscuits, and roasted chestnuts promised a good wintry lunch. Everyone was still dressed in pajamas and robes.

"Fact: Today is December twenty-sixth, Boxing Day," Mr. Wilson declared. "Did everyone enjoy Christmas yesterday? Everyone get what they wanted?" He looked expectantly through the spectacles perched on his nose.

"Why can't Christmas last all week?" Lucille pouted.

"Or all month?" her twin sister Daphne added.

"Your father's bank account would not survive a whole week of Christmas," Auntie Ei croaked. "And neither would my health." The eighty-something-year-old woman looked more exhausted than usual, having lived through another Wilson Christmas.

Stewart, one of the oldest children, nodded. "Father Christmas was good to me."

"I didn't get that motorcycle I wanted," Edward, his twin, grumbled.

"Ed, did you honestly think we would give you a motorcycle?" Mrs. Wilson asked a little sarcastically.

"Fact: You're not ready for something like that, son," Mr. Wilson said.

"But, Dad, I really want—"

"You have a job. Save your money. Buy one yourself." Mr. Wilson nodded in a finalizing way.

"I never have any money," Edward complained. "Having a girlfriend is expensive. Roly-Poly, don't ever have a girlfriend, if you can help it."

"I don't plan to any time soon." Rollie slurped up his chicken noodle soup, the only soup he liked. "I'm only twelve."

"You say that now." Stewart snickered.

"Beware of Cecily." Edward grinned.

"She's not my girlfriend! She's just my best friend."

Edward poked him in the ribs. "Whatever helps you sleep at night."

"I would like to remind everyone," Mrs. Wilson said, "that the day after tomorrow, Uncle Ky is coming for his annual visit."

Everyone cheered except for Auntie Ei, who thought it was more of an obligation than a treat to entertain her younger brother.

"Peter, he will arrive at Paddington Station at four-ten," Mrs. Wilson read from a train timetable. "Can you pick him up?"

Mr. Wilson nodded. "Does anyone want to come with me? Auntie Ei?"

"That does not sound a bit appealing," the old lady said. "He will most likely require me to drop him off when he departs—the sentimental old bean."

Though Rollie was finished eating, he waited for his father's permission to leave the table.

Mr. Wilson deliberately sighed, sipped his tea, and very slowly folded his napkin. He checked his children's empty dishes and impatient expressions. "Fact: There is still some food in your bowl, Daphne."

She studied her bare bowl. "Where, Daddy?"

"Right *there*." He pointed to a tiny bit of carrot leftover from her soup.

Daphne and Lucille erupted into a fit of giggling.

"Da-ad!" the children wailed at once.

"I guess I should know when I'm beat." He stood and blew a kiss to his wife. With a wink, he departed the dining room and headed to his personal home office for more mathematical study.

"Rollin, kindly go up to my room and fetch some letters I need mailed," Auntie Ei said. "They are on my writing desk. I will be in the library."

Rollie barreled upstairs to his great-aunt's cozy bedroom. He found a stack of addressed envelopes on her writing desk. As he scooped them up, a sheet of paper fluttered to the carpet. He snatched it up and was about to stuff it back into one of the desk's pigeonholes when he recognized Sherlock Academy's emblem on the stationery.

Without thinking, he read the letter.

20 July 1931
Lady Wilson:

I agree with the points you raised in your last letter. While I have always been interested in enrolling your great-nephew Rollin, the reasons you've given against his attending Sherlock Academy are valid. You know where I stand on the issue. If you do not wish for him to attend, I will not push the matter.
I will wait for you to decide.

Sullivan P. Yardsly

Rollie's middle fluttered as it always did when he came upon something mysterious.
Ding-Dong!
The front doorbell downstairs rang, making him jump. Quickly, Rollie stuffed the letter back into a pigeonhole in the writing desk, grabbed the envelopes to be mailed, and hurried out of the bedroom. He started downstairs. His head pounded with the confusing information in that letter.
The reasons you've given against his attending Sherlock Academy are valid.

What were these valid reasons that had led them to think that Rollie should not attend?

He paused on the landing and remembered another confusing sentence.

If you do not wish him to attend, I will not push the matter.

Why would Auntie Ei not want him to attend? And why was he now attending as if there had been no question about it? What had changed?

He reached the bottom of the stairs and inched toward the library where his great-aunt waited. She sat bundled in an armchair before the blazing fireplace. Rollie was surprised to find Headmaster Yardsly seated across from Auntie Ei.

"Ah, ROLLIN!" the headmaster hailed in his boisterous voice. "Happy Boxing Day."

"Thanks, sir, nice to see you." Rollie suddenly felt self-conscious in his pajamas.

"I assume you found them," Auntie Ei cut in, holding out her hand.

Rollie handed her the letters and stood silently by. He watched her flip through the stack with her wrinkled, crooked fingers and watched her gray eyes check the addresses. He glanced at Yardsly who was thumbing through pages in his pocket notepad.

Auntie Ei held out the three long envelopes. "Kindly put these letters in the post for me. I want them to be picked up tomorrow."

With a quick good-bye to Yardsly, Rollie took the letters. He read the addresses as he left the library: *Daily Telegraph Newspaper, Grayson and Sons Inheritance Management, Inspector Clyde of Scotland Yard.* He tugged on his boots and wrapped his black wool coat around his blue-striped pajamas. When he opened the front door, a blast of icy air made him shudder. He dashed down the front walk, almost slipping on the sleek pavement. As he plowed through the snow, he was thankful the red pillar box was just a few yards down the street from his house. He slipped the letters through the mail slot, and turned back toward home.

Quietly, he entered the house, stripped off his coat and boots, and padded over to the library door, which was open just a crack. He leaned his ear in to listen to Auntie Ei and Headmaster Yardsly's conversation. The polite side of him felt guilty for eavesdropping, but the detective side of him was curious enough to stay posted there.

"Euston is certain the MUS list is here in London," Yardsly was saying in a low tone. "We're just not sure where exactly."

"We must find that list, Sullivan," Auntie Ei replied urgently. "It contains the names of Zilch's agents and the addresses of all the MUS headquarters. Without that list, we cannot hope to bring MUS down."

"I agree, Eileen. You don't have to stress that to me—you should stress that to Scotland Yard. I need more help finding it."

"They have already reassigned the agents who were guarding Zilch's house to help you," Auntie Ei reminded him. "Which makes me nervous."

"I could still use more help—London's a large city, you know."

"I have just written to Inspector Clyde at the Yard," said Auntie Ei. "Not in regards to the MUS list, but to that other matter."

Rollie leaned in closer to the crack in the door, for he could tell by Auntie Ei's tone that she was about to divulge a secret.

"About the Will," she continued.

"Good idea. It seems Zilch is after it, as you supposed."

"His going after Watson's Case confirmed it."

"How much do you think he knows?" asked Yardsly.

Auntie Ei sighed, and Rollie could imagine her rolling her eyes. "I cannot waste my energy on speculation, but we can be certain Frederick knows more than he should."

Rollie heard a rustle and a creak and guessed the two adults were getting to their feet. Hastily, he bolted upstairs. His mind was filled with questions over the conversation he had just overheard, particularly the part about a will. In some ways, he was not surprised to learn of another mystery from Auntie Ei, for she was brimming with them. As always, there was not much chance of unlocking her secrets. At least, not right now.

He spent the rest of Boxing Day reading through the Sherlockian Encyclopedia Auntie Ei had given him for Christmas. In between lines, he pondered over the letter he had accidentally found in Auntie Ei's room. He wondered if there were more mysterious letters about him in Auntie Ei's writing desk. He had no opportunity to search for more, for she was holed up in her bedroom for the rest of the day to recuperate from Christmas. Besides, he felt uneasy about searching her bedroom; that room had always held a sort of reverence for him.

That night as he lay in bed trying to fall asleep amidst his blistering thoughts, his eyes rested on that Christmas card again. He thought about his headmaster desperately searching for the MUS list. Rollie had earned Yardsly's trust because he had now saved the Academy twice from Herr Zilch. He wished he could help track down the MUS list. He also wondered about this mysterious will Auntie Ei had mentioned that she supposed Herr Zilch was after. Who had written the will, and who was it for?

He thought about Herr Zilch eluding everyone. The villain had once been Rollie's elderly next door neighbor. Even though Zilch had told Rollie to stay out of his way and stop pursuing being a detective, Rollie had made a promise to himself to stop Zilch. He nearly had in October, but Zilch had escaped and had not been seen since. The only remnant of Zilch was his empty mansion that could be seen from Rollie's bedroom window.

BANG! BANG!

Rollie started.

With a grunt, he rolled over.

Then he squinted at a light shining through his bedroom window. His little red alarm clock pointed to 1:10 a.m.

BANG!

Now he was awake again. He stumbled over to the window and peered out.

Suddenly the light went out, the noises stopped, and the night resumed its wintry calm. The light and noises had come from Herr Zilch's vacant house. He watched another minute, and then scurried back into his toasty bed.

He wondered if what he had just witnessed really was true—it seemed a little unbelievable.

Eliot's Demands

The next day Rollie was glad to have his best friend Cecily Brighton over, partly because he was bored and partly because he needed to tell her about last night. He tried to remember what had gone on next door in the middle of the night. He had been half-asleep, but he was sure someone had turned on a light and slammed some doors. When he opened the front door for Cecily, he found her standing there with a frown. Against the white snowy backdrop, her auburn curls, green eyes, and lightly freckled nose were striking.

"Did you get a letter yet?" she asked. "From a dear friend of ours?"

Rollie checked the carpet under the front door's mail slot and picked up a few letters. One was addressed to him. As Cecily followed him back indoors, he ripped open the envelope and read the one page letter.

To Rollie:

Happy Christmas! I really hoped this would get to you on Christmas Day, but then I remembered there would be no deliveries on Christmas Day. Still, as long as it gets to you the week of Christmas, I can still wish you a Happy Christmas.

Headmaster Yardsly has given me permission to put together a team to clean Sherlock Academy. I know people usually do deep cleaning in the spring and call it spring cleaning. But since this was my idea, I get to make the rules and I think winter holiday is a great time to deep clean. I'm calling it Winter Cleaning.

I'll expect to see you at school on 29 December at ten o'clock—that should give you enough time to get over Christmas. I'll need to stay the night with you, since it's too far for me to go all the way to London and back home to Scotland in one day. Besides, I'm sure you miss me. I meant to draw you another Rollie Holmes comic strip, but ran out of time. So if you didn't have time to get me a Christmas gift, don't worry about it. See you soon!

Eliot S. Tildon

P.S. Read the back.

Rollie turned the letter over. It was blank. "He must have forgotten to write something. Are you going to help with Winter Cleaning?"

"I guess if you're going to." Cecily wiggled out of her red-and-green plaid coat and hung it on the hall tree. "There's nothing much to do now that Christmas is over. I hope Tibby goes."

"I used to love Christmas vacation when we were in regular school. But I love being at Sherlock Academy too much! I miss it."

"Me too! When I'm there, I feel like I'm always in a mystery."

"We sort of are, what with Herr Zilch always causing trouble. I've been a little worried about Wesley." Rollie's face clouded. "I haven't heard from him lately."

Last October Rollie had uncovered Herr Zilch's spy inside the Academy, a mole that turned out to be Wesley Livingston. Since Wesley had not known he was working for MUS, he had been cleared by Scotland Yard and allowed to return to school. But Wesley still feared repercussions from MUS.

While Rollie trusted Headmaster Yardsly and Scotland Yard to do their best to keep an eye on Wesley, Herr Zilch was capable of getting what he wanted no matter the obstacles. Rollie had also promised Wesley he would help protect him, and being apart from his friend made him worry. Of course Wesley could take care of himself too, for he was captain of both the rugby team and the fencing team at the Academy. Still, Rollie had now learned never to underestimate an opponent, especially when that opponent was Herr Zilch.

"Maybe he'll help with Winter Cleaning, too."

Rollie found his mother, father, and great-aunt in the library. He handed Eliot's letter to his mother. "Mum, can Eliot stay with us?"

After reading it, Mrs. Wilson smiled. "I guess we have no choice—he's already planned on it. I didn't know you volunteered to clean your school."

"We didn't," both children said in unison.

"He's in charge of the new student government, and this is his first event," Cecily explained.

"Fact: I think it's a wonderful thing to do," Mr. Wilson voiced from behind his thick volume on mathematics.

Auntie Ei spoke up. "How will you manage to get to school? Will Eliot send a hansom for you?"

"I don't know," Rollie said. "Dad, can you drive us there?"

"Fact: I can as long as it's not too snowy—I haven't prepared the car for this unexpected snow storm."

"Never mind." Auntie Ei shook her gray head. "I will ring Headmaster Yardsly and request a hansom to pick you both up on the twenty-ninth."

"Thank you, Auntie Ei."

Rollie eyed the elderly woman. He could not help feeling baffled over that letter he had discovered in her desk. What had made her question his attending the Academy last summer? What had changed?

"Eliot may stay," Mrs. Wilson consented. "We're going to have quite a full house with Uncle Ky coming too. Cecily, do you need to stay with us while your parents are away?"

Cecily shook her head. "My brother will be around. At least, he's supposed to be. He thinks he has more freedom to do what he wants when Mum and Dad are gone."

"If you need to stay with us, you're more than welcome to."

"Thanks, Mum," said Rollie as he led Cecily out of the library. He and Cecily headed upstairs to his bedroom.

"I forgot about your Uncle Ky!" said Cecily. "He's such an odd old man."

Rollie grinned. "He sure is, but he's really interesting because he's so odd. He's always got a new job. We can never keep track of his professions."

"What jobs has he had?"

"Let's see . . . he used to own a candy shop, but then he sold it and worked for a curry company. He used to compete in singing competitions in pubs. I don't know what he's doing now. Auntie Ei has never approved of how he changes jobs all the time, but he never lets her opinion stop him."

Rollie thought of telling Cecily about the letter from Yardsly to Auntie Ei that he had accidentally read. But he was not sure exactly what the letter meant, and he decided to keep it to himself until he learned more. Instead he mentioned what he had witnessed in Zilch's empty house last night.

"Are you sure you saw what you think you saw?" Cecily narrowed her eyes. "You weren't dreaming?"

"I'm pretty sure." Rollie nodded his head of sandy-blond hair. When they reached his room, he pointed through his window at the opposite window in the vacant mansion next door.

The two sleuths leaned on Rollie's desk and used his magnifying tools to spy on Herr Zilch's house. On the outside, there was no sign of a prowler. The curtains were drawn in all the windows, and the doors were barricaded with large locks and *No Trespassing* signs. Soft snow drifted in the air, erasing any footprints that might have been there.

Rollie squinted through his spyglass. He recalled the last time he had set foot in Zilch's house. It was back in August when Herr Zilch was still masquerading as his elderly neighbor Mr. Crenshaw. Rollie remembered the entry hall with vaulted ceilings painted with Italian frescos. His footsteps had echoed across the marble flooring. All the furnishings were ornate and expensive. It had seemed more like a museum than a person's home.

Zilch's secretary had answered the door and shown him in. She was young and of average height with brassy hair. She seemed to be Zilch's right hand, keeping his schedule, answering his correspondences, and traveling with him everywhere he went. Even after spying on her all summer, Rollie had never caught her name.

"Any clues?" Cecily asked, peering through the binoculars.

Rollie shook his head. "Not that I can see. If there were any footprints in the snow, they've been covered by this fresh snow falling all morning."

"The most obvious question to ask right now is who was in the house? Do you think it was a common prowler?"

"It could be, but my instincts tell me MUS has something to do with this. Maybe we should take a look around."

"Yes! There must be a secret entrance if someone got in last night," Cecily reasoned. Her face clouded as she added, "But then if it's someone involved with MUS, he probably has a key to get in."

Rollie shook his head. "No, he wouldn't. Those locks on the doors belong to Scotland Yard. They locked up the house after they searched it when Zilch escaped last summer."

"Good! Then there is another way the prowler's getting in, and we will get in another way too!" Cecily headed for the door.

"Let's wait and see if the prowler returns," Rollie suggested. "I don't want to trespass unless we have a really good reason. I'll stay up tonight and keep watch. Maybe we can learn some more."

They spied on the vacant house a little longer before they agreed there was nothing more they could do about this new mystery until Rollie had a chance to confirm the prowler later that night.

"You know what this reminds me of?" Cecily pointed to the mansion. "Sherlock Holmes' case *The Adventure of the Empty House.*"

"That's my favorite case!" exclaimed Rollie. "I haven't read it since I put my Holmes volume in the Rearranging Library. I like that case because it's the first one Holmes tackles after his hiatus for three years. Everyone thought he died at Reichenbach Falls with Moriarty. He returns alive and shocks everyone. He and Watson stake out an empty house next to 221 Baker Street to catch Moriarty's last minion, Colonel Sebastian Moran."

"And Holmes puts a lifelike bust of himself in his own window to make Moran think he's at home hanging out," Cecily added excitedly.

"He had Mrs. Hudson hide in his flat to turn the bust every few minutes so it looked like he was moving around," Rollie remembered.

"Good ol' Mrs. Hudson! She was the best housekeeper anyone could ever ask for. Even though Holmes was just her tenant, she looked after him and helped him with his cases. She even went with him when he retired to Sussex to keep bees."

Rollie continued. "Yet Holmes didn't tell her that he had survived his mortal combat with Moriarty at Reichenback Falls in Switzerland. He kept it a secret—even from Watson!"

Cecily shrugged. "You know he had to for his own safety. And it made Holmes intriguing. People are more interesting when they have a secret."

Rollie looked at her, his brown eyes widening. "Really? So do you have a secret?"

"Hmm, not that I can think of. Christmas is over, so I don't have to keep any more secrets about gifts. How about you?"

Rollie grimaced, and proceeded to tell her about the letter from Yardsly to Auntie Ei. Cecily encouraged him to talk to Auntie Ei about it, but Rollie was not so sure yet. He felt frustrated about Auntie Ei's secret-keeping, and not just about the contents of that letter, but also about his family lineage she had mentioned in October. He had not been able to learn anything new from her about that. And now there was this secret of a will she was keeping, too.

"Cecily, if you had a secret, would you tell me?"

"Of course I would. We're comrades, after all. We have been since first grade."

Rollie smiled, remembering the first day of first grade. Cecily and her family had moved in a few weeks before school started. He had been excited when new neighbors moved in and had hoped there would be new children to play with. He had been slightly disappointed when his new neighbor turned out to be a girl—a bossy girl, no less.

It was not until they were lined up to enter their classroom that Rollie and Cecily had met. Cecily wore a pink frilly dress and a pout on her freckled face.

On the verge of tears, she whispered, "I *hate* wearing dresses!"

Rollie glanced at her and thought she looked pretty. "But you're a girl."

Cecily gave him the biggest glare. "Take that back! Or I won't be your friend!"

"I don't want to be your friend!" he had shouted back.

The rest of their first day, they had avoided each other. But somehow, they always found themselves stealing glances at each other, though neither would have admitted it. When they were heading home, she discovered they lived just two houses apart.

"We have to be friends." Cecily decided, hurrying to catch up with Rollie. "We're neighbors and we're the only children on this street. We'll be so bored without each other."

Rollie hated to admit that she was right. "Fine. We'll be friends."

It was settled. From that day on, their friendship had grown with their heights. After Auntie Ei had introduced Rollie to Sherlock Holmes, he had introduced the detective to Cecily. She immediately shared Rollie's fascination with all things Holmes. Now Rollie could not imagine his life without her.

"Rollie?" Cecily brought him back from his memories. "Let me know what happens tonight with the prowler. I hope he shows up again."

"I do too."

Two Failures

Rollie sat at his desk to watch the dark, deserted house through his frosted window. He hoped tonight would bring back the mysterious prowler.

Rollie had no problem being up at night. He had made several midnight excursions at Sherlock Academy of Fine Sleuths while working on cases. At first, his middle had fluttered and his nerves had been on edge. But now he had grown accustomed to the noises native to the dead of night, which most people never heard. Of course being at home this time was a great comfort. Still, he noticed the night.

The large Wilson manor settled with creaks and groans. The radiator down in the hall rumbled on and off. Somewhere out in the back garden an owl hooted. The faithful ticking of his little red alarm clock kept him friendly company and kindly reminded him of the passing minutes.

When he felt his eyelids drooping closed, Rollie glanced at the little clock. In the moonlight, he saw it was nearly two. He groaned. The prowler had shown up around one last night. Rollie was afraid the prowler was not coming. He got up from the desk and paced his small room, forcing his blood to circulate. He shivered but resisted wrapping a blanket around himself, knowing this would only make him sleepier.

Twenty minutes passed. Nothing. Another ten passed, and still nothing.

Rollie gave in. He dragged one of the quilts off his bed, wrapped it around himself, and settled down at his desk again. Part of him doubted he had seen that light or heard those noises last night, but he had definitely been awakened. There had been no activity of any kind next door since Herr Zilch had fled in August—as far as Rollie knew. He was only home on the weekends though. Perhaps someone had been rummaging through the vacant house during all those weeks Rollie was away studying to be a detective like the great Holmes. But then he figured no one would have tampered with the house since it had been under the surveillance of a Scotland Yard team . . . which had recently been called off . . . interesting . . .

Rollie blinked his eyes open and read his Christmas card from his teachers again. Just like their unique signatures, the teachers had such unique personalities.

Miss Gwendolyn A. Gram's cursive signature was flowery like herself. She taught Spy Etiquette and Interrogation. Rollie cared the least for her for all the same reasons the girls at school adored her: she was young and fashionable, and she was dating his favorite teacher, Mr. Chad. Mr. Chad had signed his name in quick capital letters. Rollie loved Mr. Chad's American accent, sense of humor, and disguise lessons.

Rollie drowsily checked the clock. It was two-thirty.

Back to the Christmas card. Ms. Katherine E. Yardsly, the headmaster's younger sister who taught code-cracking, had signed her name backwards to be read in a mirror. Then there was Miss Amelia S. Hertz who loved to analyze finger and footprints, so a thumbprint acted as her signature on the card. Mr. Percy E. Notch, who trained the students how to be effective observers, had left his mark with scribbles that Rollie assumed represented his name.

Two forty-five.

Then there was Headmaster Sullivan P. Yardsly; he had signed his name with his initials, which Rollie noticed for the first time spelled *SPY*. Headmaster Yardsly resembled Sherlock Holmes. He was tall and lean with a receding hairline, prominent forehead, and hawk-like nose. Yardsly had commissioned Rollie to help solve the mysteries involving Herr Zilch in the past. He knew the headmaster was glad he was a student at Sherlock Academy . . .

. . . Even if Auntie Ei had not wanted him to be.

Three o'clock.

Rollie could not forget that line Yardsly had written to his great-aunt. *The reasons you've given against his attending Sherlock Academy are valid.*

What else did the letter say?

He couldn't remember. He needed to read that letter one more time. Now would be a good time to go find it . . . But should he?

He stood up. He sat down.

No, he would not search Auntie Ei's room. Besides, he would not be able to see in her dark room—using a flashlight was out of the question. And he could not abandon his post by the window. He would try tomorrow. Maybe during breakfast he could make an excuse . . . go upstairs . . . look for . . . the . . .

He shook his head to awaken himself.

As he followed his thoughts, they led him down a winding path of *what ifs*.

What if he could find the MUS list? This would help Yardsly track down and arrest MUS agents hiding undercover in Great Britain. This would break Britain's premier crime ring and protect Sherlock Academy. This would defeat Herr Zilch.

Rollie grew excited. Where could the list be? Where would Zilch have hidden it?

Rollie looked out his window at the dark mansion. Could it be there? What if the prowler was looking for it?

He had to find that list. He had a hunch it could be right next door . . . or maybe it was just a wish. Either way, it would not hurt to take a look around . . . tomorrow . . . maybe he and Cecily . . . could . . .

*   *   *   *

The gray light of dawn startled him. Rollie blinked around, confused at first that he was slumped over his desk and not lying in his bed. Then he remembered the reason but did not remember falling asleep.

The red clock showed him seven ten.

"Oh, drat!"

He hoped that the prowler had not shown up while he was asleep. A bright light or slamming doors surely would have woken him like the first time. Feeling annoyed with himself, he fell onto his bed, burrowed beneath the covers, and dosed back off.

A banging door did wake him, but this time it was a family member—probably his mother who was always the first to rise. Next would be Auntie Ei and his seven-year-old sisters. His father and his teenage brothers would battle for last place. Mr. Wilson thought it was his right to sleep in on holiday, for he was up early the rest of the year to teach math at Regent's College. Rollie's brothers thought they were entitled to sleep in because they were still growing teenagers. And Rollie always woke up somewhere in between everyone else, reminding the family there was one more person in the house.

He rolled out of bed and shrugged into his robe. He traipsed down to the second floor. As he neared

Auntie Ei's closed door, he halted. He pressed his ear to the door.

Auntie Ei threw open the door. "Rollin, what on earth are you doing outside my door?" she exclaimed.

"I was just, um, checking if you, uh, were up," Rollie stammered.

"How very peculiar!" Auntie Ei closed the door behind her and led him downstairs. "I do hope this school holiday is not dulling your intelligence."

Rollie swallowed. "I think I'm onto a case." He quickly caught her up on his suspicions about Zilch's mansion, the MUS list, and the night prowler. When he was finished, he expected Auntie Ei to give her usual affirmation, or perhaps her own thoughts on the matter.

"You will not find anything there," she said bluntly. "Scotland Yard thoroughly searched the house and found nothing of importance. Do not waste your time on it."

"But what about the prowler?"

"Perhaps it was just a prowler, nothing more. However, it would not hurt to keep an eye on the property. We may need to notify the police." With a curt nod, she led him into the dining room.

They found a warm breakfast of porridge, crumpets, and Rollie's favorite hash browns ready for them on the table. Mrs. Wilson hollered her husband's and sons' names for a few minutes until everyone joined them.

"Fact: I think this morning was a tie between us." Mr. Wilson chuckled, pointing to the twin boys.

"What do you mean, Dad? I'm still asleep." Edward yawned. "Ouch!"

Lucille pinched her brother and giggled.

He tickled her back.

"Stop it, Ed!"

"You snore so loudly!" Daphne shared with everyone. "Does he keep you awake, Stew?"

Stewart shrugged. "I've gotten used to it after sharing a room with him all my life."

"You're always quiet," Edward noted in between bites of his porridge.

"Compared to you, everybody's quiet," joked Stewart.

"That may be perhaps," Auntie Ei said, "the first sensible thing you have observed, young man."

"Thank you, old woman," Stewart returned, chewing on a crumpet.

"Don't be cheeky!" Mrs. Wilson scolded.

"Nonsense! I appreciate his candor." Auntie Ei rolled her eyes sarcastically.

Rollie took a bite of hash browns, his only breakfast ever, and asked, "Dad, may I be excused? I need to use the loo."

Mr. Wilson nodded without glancing up from his newspaper. "More unseasonable snow predicted for the next few days."

Rollie left the dining room, avoiding Auntie Ei's suspicious look. He jogged upstairs, but instead of going to the bathroom, he stopped by Auntie Ei's bedroom. He rarely entered her bedroom, and only by invitation. His heart pounded, and he almost walked away. But a desperate curiosity to know more about that letter urged him to turn the doorknob.

Quietly, he slipped into the room, and rummaged through her desk. He carefully moved around the mail, pens, ink well, blotter, and stationery. There was no trace of the letter from Headmaster Yardsly. Had Auntie Ei hidden it away, thinking he had found it earlier? He did find lots of newspaper clippings stuffed in the pigeonholes. The initials MUS caught his attention.

Jewel Thief Strikes Again! Believed to be Tied to MUS!

King's Cross Murder Believed to Be the Work of MUS!

Tourists Warned to Guard Their Pockets Against MUS Pick-Pocketers in Trafalgar Square!

Scotland Yard Doubles Efforts to Track Down MUS Spies Near Baker Street.

"ROLLIN! HOW DARE YOU SEARCH THROUGH MY PERSONAL PROPERTY!"

Rollie jumped and his stomach flipped.

"I respect you as a detective, but you have crossed a line—invading my private bedroom! What are you searching for?"

Rollie gulped. "A letter you have from Headmaster Yardsly. It's about me."

Auntie Ei's mouth tightened and she narrowed her eyes, defining her wrinkles even more. "Why do you want that letter?"

"Because it's about me! You're keeping secrets from me! Why?"

"There are many secrets I am obliged to keep, and some of them do concern you. I will share them with you all in good time." Auntie Ei drew herself up. "Now is not the time."

"I don't understand you." Rollie could feel his face heating up with anger and his heart pounding with hurt. "I hate that you keep secrets from me."

"That makes no difference to me." Her shoulders twitched as if she almost shrugged, but she resisted the unladylike behavior. "I believe you owe me an apology for ransacking my desk."

Rollie knew she was right, but he was not about to let her get away so easily. "I deserve to know your secrets about me."

Auntie Ei practically glared at him. "As your elder, I am not obligated to disclose anything to you, nor do you deserve any explanation. Do you understand, young man?"

Rollie huffed, and before he could stop himself, he shot back, "Yes, *old woman!*"

He ran out and stomped upstairs to his room. While Stewart could get away with snide remarks, he knew he could not due to the special bond he shared with Auntie Ei. He was out of line calling her old woman and searching her bedroom; he could hardly believe he had just done both. But he did not return to apologize, for she had insulted his judgment as a detective and had hurt him with her secrecy.

Rollie stayed in his room while the rest of the family finished breakfast. He had no appetite, and he could not face Auntie Ei at the table. To pass the time, he checked on the vacant house. He made his bed and tidied the room. After getting dressed, he sat on the floor and updated his bookshelf. He took two Hardy Boys books off his shelf marked *Excellent Books, My Favorites*. This made room for his new Sherlockian Encyclopedia from Auntie Ei.

He frowned.

Finally, his growling stomach drove him in search of lunch downstairs. As he neared the kitchen, he heard a commotion of slamming doors, stamping feet, and appalled voices. In the kitchen, he was shocked at the group of people he found there—one person in particular.

Outsmarting MUS

"Wesley!" Rollie tackled his friend.

"Hallo, mate!" Wesley laughed. The tall fourteen-year-old boy flashed a smile of perfect teeth, and pulled his blue knit cap off his short brown hair. On his brow, he sported a fresh bump. "Happy Christmas!"

Rollie pointed to the bruise. "What happened to your forehead?"

"From the attack." Wesley's deep brown eyes revealed a tinge of fear.

"What attack?" Rollie asked. "What's going on? Why are you here?"

Wesley was not alone. With him was a man dressed in a long, black coat. He stood at an average height, and even in his winter coat, he was slim. An aged scar on his right cheek drew most of

Rollie's attention. He kept peeking out the kitchen window, barely separating the curtains. His beady eyes swiftly swept the back garden then turned to scope the kitchen.

"Who are you?" Mrs. Wilson demanded of the young man.

"I am Euston Hood. I work with Sullivan Yardsly." Euston handed Mrs. Wilson a slip of paper. "A few instructions from Headmaster Yardsly."

Mrs. Wilson read the brief note and turned to Rollie. "Your headmaster would like us to board Wesley for safekeeping."

"Can he stay, Mum?" Rollie asked excitedly.

"I suppose, although I don't quite understand everything. Let me tell your father . . . Peter!" She went in search of her husband.

Euston turned to the two boys. "Wesley, you will stay with the Wilsons and return to school on January eighteenth. If there is any trouble, contact the Academy. Rollin—"

"Call me Rollie."

"Thanks. I would advise you to keep to the house. Don't take Wesley into the city."

"What about Winter Cleaning tomorrow?" Rollie asked. "At school?"

Euston looked confused. "I don't know anything about that, but if you're only going to the Academy and back, I'm sure that would be fine."

"Does Headmaster have any clues to find Herr Zilch?"

"We've confirmed Wesley's attack did come from MUS," Euston answered, lowering his voice. "Headmaster is following up a lead in Brighton and Hove. I must catch the next train from Victoria Station to meet him there. We'll be in touch." He nodded curtly and stepped to the door. After a careful look outside, he slipped out of the house.

"I'm so glad you're staying with us," Rollie told his friend.

"Me too! It will be way more fun than being home alone." Wesley picked up his suitcase and followed Rollie upstairs to his bedroom. "And I'll feel safer."

"Tell me about the attack."

Wesley opened his suitcase while Rollie cleared out a drawer in his bureau.

"I've never been more scared before in my life!" Wesley admitted.

"What happened?"

"Let me begin by first explaining what happened before Christmas vacation. My parents were

38

really concerned about everything that happened in October. I had to beg them to let me stay enrolled at Sherlock Academy. They weren't sure it was the best place for me anymore. But Headmaster argued for me. He assured my parents that he would do everything to keep me safe and that it would be a great loss for me and everyone else if I dropped out. So Mother and Father agreed to let me stay in school."

"I'm glad to hear that. I would miss you a lot, and so would the rugby and fencing teams."

"Thanks, mate," Wesley said. "Which reminds me: I can't forget to turn in my tuition money for this next semester. Did you mail yours in or give it to Headmaster?"

Rollie shrugged. "Someone else has been paying my tuition—someone anonymous. It's very mysterious."

"That *is* mysterious. Anyways, Christmas vacation came. And there was a big debate over what to do with me. Headmaster thought I should stay at school all vacation to be safe from MUS and under his watchful eye. My parents thought I'd be safer at home under *their* watchful eyes. I didn't really know where I'd be safer—I just knew I'd be bored at either place with all my friends gone home. Finally,

Headmaster consented to my going home, and my parents consented to having Euston come along to keep an eye on me.

"The first couple days home, everything seemed fine. My parents and I got ready for Christmas. My older sister, Olivia, came home from Cambridge. Euston kept watch. Then a few days before Christmas, something strange happened. Well, it seemed normal at first but turned out to be strange.

"We noticed a uniformed policeman patrolling the street corner a few houses down from us. We had never seen a bobby there before, so we mentioned it to Euston. He promised to keep an eye on him. My father thought perhaps because it was Christmas, the police were keeping an extra watchful eye on our neighborhood to ward off thieves. The bobby would stand on the corner for a few hours, leave for a few hours, then return for a few more hours. His schedule seemed very erratic. Finally on Christmas Eve, Euston decided to confront the bobby.

"As Euston headed down the sidewalk toward him, the bobby quickly left his corner. Euston wanted to follow him but knew it was more important to guard us. So he returned to our house. He telephoned the local police station and asked about the bobby. The police station denied sending anyone to patrol our neighborhood. That's when we knew this so-called bobby was an imposter. And, of course, we guessed he was an MUS agent.

"Christmas came and went without interruption. On Boxing Day, Olivia left to meet some friends in Greece on holiday. Father and Mother got called back to Belgium for their export-import business—they're business partners, so they always travel together. They wanted me to go with them. I didn't really want to—it's so dull traveling with them when they're on business. I was glad that Euston agreed I should stay because it would be harder for him to watch over me while traveling. So my parents reluctantly left me at home with Euston.

"We hadn't seen any sign of that bobby since he ran away from Euston. So Euston and I started to feel better. He joined me for meals, and he played a game of chess with me once. I also learned something very interesting about him—remind me to tell you when I'm done with this story. Most of the time, he was out keeping watch, which meant I was cooped up inside without much to do.

"Yesterday Headmaster rang me to see how things were going. He invited me to go back to the

Academy while my parents were away. He said I could hang out with Rupert and Margot and help with some odd jobs around the school. That sounded way more fun than what I was doing at home—which was nothing. Euston agreed to take me to London that very morning.

"And that's when the attack happened. Euston wanted to send my parents a telegram about what we were doing. I still needed to pack. Euston didn't want to leave me, but I assured him I would be fine. The telegraph office was just down the street. Besides, we hadn't seen anything suspicious since that bobby ran away.

"A few minutes after Euston left, there was a knock on the front door. I peeked through the window beside the door and didn't see anyone outside, but I saw a package on the front porch. I opened the door and read the label. It was addressed to my next-door neighbor, Mr. Twiddle. It had accidentally been delivered to my house instead—this has happened before.

"Since I was leaving, I thought I had better deliver it to Mr. Twiddle. Otherwise he would never get it. I took the package next door and left it on his doormat. On my way back home, a black auto suddenly stopped next to me. Two men leapt out and tried to drag me into the back seat! I hit my head on the car as they tried to force me in."

"What did you do?" Rollie asked, wide-eyed.

"I gave one of them a rugby head-butt, and the other I kicked in the shins. I don't think they were expecting a fight from me. They loosened their grip on me for a second—that's all I needed! I ran away as fast as I could.

"Behind me, I could hear their footsteps chasing after me, and I heard the car's tires screech as it joined in the chase. I reached my house, barged in, and locked the door behind me. I stood frozen in the hall, my heart pounding. I wasn't sure my locked front door was enough to keep them out. They seemed desperate to get me.

"I waited a few seconds but didn't hear anything. Finally I got up the courage to peek through the window. The black car was gone, and so were the two men in suits. Instead Euston was running up to my front door.

"He banged on the door. 'Mr. Livingston, are you in there? Are you alright?' he shouted.

"I had never heard him shout before or heard such panic in his voice. I quickly threw open the door and assured him I was fine. He pointed out my bruised forehead."

Wesley fingered the bump.

"It was MUS. Euston said that just as he came out of the telegraph office. He saw the car and the men in suits chasing me. As he ran after the men, they hopped into the car and sped off. He decided it was more important to check on me than to pursue the car. Neither of us could read the license plates.

"Euston immediately rang Headmaster. They both agreed that my life was in more danger than they had anticipated. They agreed that not even Sherlock Academy would be safe enough for me—and staying home was not an option. That's when Headmaster came up with the idea for me to stay with you. I have to say, I got really excited about staying with you!

"Euston and I boarded the express train for London. Euston never left my side and was more watchful than ever. I finally realized what a good secret agent he is. When we got to London, we switched taxis and buses as well as changed routes and directions several times. I started to get dizzy! Finally we reached the Primrose Hill suburbs and I knew we were close to your house. The taxi let us out down the street, and we walked the rest of the way here. Euston's eyes were everywhere, and his grip never let go of my shoulder. We sneaked through your garden gate and Euston covered our tracks in the snow. I felt relief when we entered your kitchen. And here I am for your safekeeping.

"I told you Herr Zilch would come for me. I'm still so sorry, Rollie."

"For what?" Rollie asked.

"This is all my fault," Wesley said. "If I hadn't been so gullible enough to be used by Zilch, you wouldn't have had to stop me. And I wouldn't be putting you in danger with me."

"I would have stopped Zilch's mole no matter who it had been," Rollie replied. "I would still be in this danger whether you were involved or not."

Wesley nodded. "I'm just having a hard time letting it all go."

"You can't let the past drag you down." Rollie patted his shoulder. "Why do you think Zilch wants to kidnap you?"

Wesley threw up his hands in exasperation. "Revenge! To get back at me for betraying him. Why else? He can't be afraid of my letting out his secrets—I don't know anything!"

"Are you scared?"

Wesley frowned. "To be totally honest with you, I am now. Zilch seems to be everywhere and seems to know everything. That scares me. How about you?"

"Back in October, I made a promise to myself to stop him no matter the cost. I felt pretty brave. Now I'm not so sure of myself. My great-aunt who I thought believed in me as a detective has turned out to think the opposite about me. And now you've had a close call with MUS."

Wesley gripped Rollie's shoulder. "Well, at least we're in this together, right, mate?"

"Right!" Rollie grinned. "So what did you learn about Euston?"

"When we played chess, it was the first time he rolled up his sleeves. I noticed he was wearing a leather wristband with a strange symbol etched on it. I asked him about it. He told me he belongs to an undercover society that had been established to specifically fight MUS."

"Really? What's the secret society called?"

Wesley grinned. "The Holmes Brigade."

Return of the Prowler

Rollie perked with interest. "The Holmes Brigade! Who's in it? What are their duties?"

Wesley shrugged. "Euston didn't say much— one of his annoying habits. But I definitely plan on asking him more about it. So what did you get for Christmas?"

Rollie showed him his new rugby ball from his father, a Holmes-like coat his mother had sewn, and the Sherlockian Encyclopedia from his great-aunt. Wesley was interested in all three gifts.

"Nice ball for some rugby drills. I gotta whip you back into shape, mate." Wesley always looked for opportunities to improve Rollie's skills in rugby. "This coat matches your deerstalker hat."

"Yep, my mum was able to find similar fabric to match it." Rollie put on his Holmes hat that he had received as a special award from Yardsly for stopping Herr Zilch the first time.

Wesley sat on the edge of Rollie's bed and untied his black Converse sneakers. "It wasn't snowing in Brighton, so I didn't think of wearing my boots. These need to dry."

"I haven't been able to wear my Converse you gave me since we've been on holiday. We haven't had snow like this in ages!"

Wesley ran his eyes over Rollie's desk crammed with spying tools. "So, detective, are there any cases you're working on right now?"

"Well . . . " Rollie filled Wesley in on what he and Cecily had been secretly working on regarding Zilch's list of agents and headquarters, and the prowler at the vacant house. He decided to also tell him about his fight with Auntie Ei, just so Wesley would know why he was not talking to the elderly woman.

"Hallo, detectives," Cecily announced as she entered Rollie's room. "Wesley, what are you doing here?"

"Staying here for safekeeping. Happy Christmas."

To Rollie's confusion, Cecily blushed. He wondered what she had to be embarrassed about.

Rollie told her, "We were just discussing the mystery at Zilch's vacant house. We should wait and see if anyone returns. As far as I know, no one showed up last night."

"But if someone does return, we can go over there and explore, right?" Cecily pressed. "What do you think, Wesley?"

"Absolutely, but Euston wants me to stay here as much as possible."

"Euston? Is he the chap who met Rupert in the park for information?" Cecily asked. "Rupert mentioned him."

Wesley nodded. "He's Yardsly's inside man. Euston has a lot of knowledge on Herr Zilch and MUS. He's the one who confirmed that there was a list of MUS agents and their headquarters."

"What are we going to do about this case?" Cecily jumped back to the pressing topic.

"Nothing—until tonight." Rollie shrugged.

"I hope you don't mind, but I've got a lot of Independent Study homework to catch up on," Wesley said as he dug out a folder of papers from his suitcase.

"I haven't worked on mine at all," Rollie admitted.

"Me neither." Cecily sighed. "I guess now would be a good time to get some work done. Can I borrow your syllabus Rollie, so I don't have to go home?"

Rollie nodded and started searching for his Independent Study folder. He found it in his top desk drawer. The three friends sat on the floor to work on their English, math, science, and social studies homework assigned over vacation.

"I wish we could work on detective homework instead of this homework," mumbled Rollie as he diagramed a sentence.

"Me, too," Cecily said. "I'd much rather be updating my observation notes. I'm still working on Miss Gram's profile. I have a profile on every teacher at school, you know."

Wesley looked up with interest. "That's impressive. Observation class is my worst subject. I'm too active to sit still and observe for very long."

"Cecily's observations have helped in many cases," Rollie bragged. "They're how we figured out you were the mole."

"And that Lady Gram was not the secretary, though she reminded us of the secretary. Oh goodness!" Cecily suddenly gasped. "I forgot about all those notes we kept on Zilch when he was Mr. Crenshaw last summer!"

"I did too! We should read through them for any extra clues."

Wesley grinned. "I guess it does pay off to be observant."

* * * *

Around five that evening, Mr. Wilson returned home with Uncle Ky. While Wesley and Cecily continued to work on their Independent Studies upstairs, Rollie hurried down to greet his great-uncle.

Lord Kylen Wilson was tall and thin, his frame exaggerated by the baggy dark green three-piece suit he wore. From his waistcoat, a gold watch chain dangled. He was mainly bald atop his head, but the white hair left around his head was fluffy and a little unkempt. His gray eyes were deep set beneath equally unkempt white eyebrows. He shared one feature with his older sister Eileen: a sharp nose that he twitched often.

The family surrounded him in the entry hall to take turns giving him a welcoming hug. Rollie joined them, being sure to stand as far away from Auntie Ei as he could.

"Oh, hello, Rollin, how are you?" Uncle Ky inquired in his mumbly way. He patted the boy on his sandy-blond head.

"Good, thank you, Uncle Ky."

"Good, good. I see you've grown a bit. That's good." Uncle Ky stuck his hands in his pockets and jingled the loose change around. "I hear you're attending Sherlock Academy, eh?"

"Yes, I just started this year."

"You're enjoying it—the Academy?"

"I love it!"

"Has your Auntie Ei been showing you the ropes around the place?"

Auntie Ei drew herself up taller. "Certainly not, Kylen! The boy must learn to stand on his own two feet."

Rollie cast his eyes to the floor.

Uncle Ky laughed, or at least it appeared he did. When he laughed, he never made any noise, but his shoulders shook.

"What job do you have right now?" Rollie could not wait to ask.

Uncle Ky's shoulders shook again. "Nothing too exciting, you know. I'm the official clock master at Christ Church University in Oxford. My job is to keep all the clocks running properly. There are quite a few to look after, you know."

"Fact: That sounds like quite a job!" Mr. Wilson said.

"I suppose. It can be painfully dull, keeping time." Uncle Ky jingled his coins again. "Universities are quite stuffy, you know. But it keeps me busy. What do you think of that, Eileen? Is this finally a job you approve of?"

Auntie Ei gave a curt nod. "It is a fine job, to be sure. I am only happy you finally landed something admirable and steady."

"I'll see how long I last." Uncle Ky shrugged. "You know I'm not a big gift-giver, but I did pick up a little something for you, Rollin." He dug around in his coat pocket and fished out a small parcel, which he handed to Rollie. "Just a little trinket I thought you might fancy now that you're in the line of detective work."

Rollie opened the small box. Inside glistened two shiny silver whistles.

"Policeman's whistles—you know, the kind bobbies use to alert for trouble. I started collecting them and thought you may want one for yourself and a comrade. I have a whole case of them, if you would care to see some time. I used to collect clocks, but I sold the lot after taking on this clock master position."

"Thank you, Uncle Ky, they're great!"

"I am sure you are weary from your travels," Mrs. Wilson said. "Would you like to freshen up before supper?"

"Oh, yes, that would be lovely. Usually it takes only about an hour from Oxford to London, you know. But there was a derailment at Reading because of all this snow. Quite unusual this time of year, all this snow." Uncle Ky grabbed his suitcase.

"Why don't you visit more often since you're only an hour away?" Mr. Wilson asked.

Uncle Ky glanced at his sister with a twinkle in his eyes. "I think Eileen can tolerate only one visit from me a year, right ol' bird?"

* * *

Later that night, Rollie took the first shift since Wesley was tired from a day of traveling and dodging MUS. On the floor, Wesley slept in a sleeping bag borrowed from Edward. He breathed quietly, which Rollie appreciated because his roommates at school were always snoring. Now that he thought about them, he was looking forward to seeing Eliot and Rupert the next day for Winter Cleaning.

Rollie settled down in his desk chair to keep watch over Zilch's mansion. He was determined to stay awake this time, at least through his assigned shift. He would wake Wesley at three.

He had two more hours to go.

BAM!

Rollie jolted. He squinted as a bright light shone from that same second floor window of the mansion next door.

"Wesley, wake up!" He shook his friend sleeping on the floor.

Without missing a beat, Wesley sat bolt upright and dove for the window. The boys watched a distorted silhouette move behind the closed drapes. Then it was gone.

BAM!

"The prowler must be in another room," Wesley concluded. "He sure likes to slam doors." He looked through the binoculars. "I can't see much through that drape."

"I wish it wasn't closed," Rollie agreed

The distorted silhouette returned.

"He's back!" Rollie shouted.

The prowler seemed average height and was wearing a bulky coat and knit cap. The person kept exiting the room and returning every few minutes with objects in his arms. After about ten minutes of this, the light went out. There was one more door slammed, and then all was silent.

Wesley turned this way and that, still peering through the binoculars. "Where did he exit? I don't see anyone on this side. No footprints either."

"The entrance must be on the other side of the house."

Wesley set the binoculars down and scooted back into his sleeping bag on the floor. He whispered, "We should find a way in and open those drapes. That way we'll see everything that goes on when the prowler returns."

"We might as well explore the house too and see if there's anything of interest. It looked like the prowler was bringing things into the room."

"I agree. Tomorrow—"

"Wait!" Rollie said. "We have Winter Cleaning tomorrow."

"Will it take all day?"

"Who knows what Eliot has planned?"

"We should try to get back before dark. If not, I guess we'll have to wait until Friday. 'Night, mate."

Rollie smiled, glad his best buddy was staying with him, glad Wesley was safe with the Wilsons, and glad to have a case to think about again. His instincts told him a mystery was brewing next door. He hoped their investigation could help Yardsly and Euston track down Herr Zilch. Ultimately, he hoped Zilch's list was somewhere in the vacant mansion. He knew there were risks involved, especially with a prowler on the loose, and especially if that prowler was Zilch's agent.

Rollie had always known Herr Zilch and MUS were dangerous, but Wesley's attack had made the danger feel closer, more personal. It reminded Rollie that Zilch was not to be trifled with and that the villain could be close.

In the past, Rollie had found courage in Auntie Ei's support. Knowing that she believed in him as a detective and supported his attending Sherlock Academy had given him the added courage to stand up against Herr Zilch. But according to the letter he had found in her desk, she thought otherwise. This made him feel differently about himself and about fighting Zilch.

He only hoped his own confidence in himself would be enough to combat the creeping fear of Herr Zilch.

And he secretly hoped the cost of being a young detective would not be too steep.

Another Secret in the Library

The hansom arrived at nine thirty the next morning to pick up Rollie, Wesley, and Cecily. Sherlock Academy's taxi service was comprised of single horse-drawn hansoms, the same kind that Sherlock Holmes had often used in Victorian London. A driver tipped his bowler hat and assisted the children into the two-seater cab. Since Cecily was the smallest, she sat sandwiched between the boys, a little more red than usual coloring her cheeks.

The driver climbed up to his perch behind them and flicked the reins. The chestnut horse *crunchety-crunched* down the snowy lane. Soon the hansom left the quiet suburbs of Primrose Lane and entered the busy city of London proper. Many stores and businesses were closed for the holiday week, but the famous beastly London traffic still clogged the narrow streets. Red double-decker buses roared past them, and automobiles, mostly black taxis, honked in warning at the antique hansom.

"How did the stakeout go last night?" Cecily asked, seemingly not sure which boy to turn to first.

Rollie and Wesley caught her up on the prowler's return and on their plan to open the drape.

"Here be 221 Baker Street!" the hansom driver hollered.

He pulled the horse to a halt, hopped down, and opened the door for them with a tip of his bowler hat. The three friends scrambled out. The tall red brick building looked lonely, for the windows were dark and snow was piled a few feet high against the front double doors. A notice was posted by the doorbell: *On Holiday. School will resume the third week of January.*

Rollie and Wesley dug their feet into the slush and plowed it aside from the door. Finding the door unlocked, they entered Sherlock Academy. The warm, cozy building was unusually calm. Green garlands bedecked with red ornaments drooped sleepily from the banister. Stacks of unread newspapers sagged in the corners. The halls were empty, taking a vacation from trampling students. All was so quiet they could hear the ticking of the grandfather clock from its position near the stairs and the rumbling of the radiator down the hall. A tinge of gingerbread scented the air. Standing there, Rollie felt a little school-sick again.

"WHO'S THERE?" a familiar voiced boomed from the office off the entry hall.

Wesley led the other two into Headmaster's office, which had once been the living quarters of Holmes and his trusty comrade, Dr. Watson. A generous fire roared in the fireplace, shedding an orange glow upon the two armchairs and the bearskin rug before it.

"HAPPY HOLIDAYS! I trust you had a good Christmas."

Headmaster Sullivan P. Yardsly sat in Holmes' sunken leather armchair. Papers littered his lap. With his long, thin fingers, he beckoned the visitors in. His tall, lean figure was clothed in a burgundy dress robe, much like the one Holmes would have worn to lounge about in.

"I assume you're here for Eliot's Winter Cleaning?" Yardsly asked.

"I thought you were in Brighton, sir," Wesley said in surprise.

"I got back at dawn." Dark circles beneath his eyes were proof of his escapades. "I'm glad to see you safe and sound. Hello, Cecily. Rollin, thank you for taking Wesley in."

"I'm happy to, sir." Rollie nodded.

"WELL! You'll find Eliot and a few other students in the teachers' lounge. HAPPY CLEANING!"

The three students headed out of the office.

"ROLLIN! A word with you." Yardsly beckoned him back to the fire.

As Wesley and Cecily headed down the hall, Rollie sank into Watson's armchair across from his headmaster.

"Would you mind doing me a favor, lad? The secret library needs to be dusted and tidied." Yardsly lowered his voice. "You're the only student who knows about it. Could you be in charge of that?"

Rollie's brown eyes sparkled. "I would love to!"

"GOOD! Be sure to lock yourself in the library, so other students don't see you cleaning the secret shelves. You'll need the marmalade jars, of course. They're all in that cupboard." Yardsly pointed to a little wooden cabinet mounted on the wall next to his desk.

Rollie jumped to his feet. "I better check in with Eliot first, so he doesn't come looking for me.

I'll be back in a minute." He started to leave but paused. "Sir, did you have any luck tracing MUS in Brighton?"

Yardsly rubbed his eyes. "WELL, I found the black auto they used—a four-door Bently. It had been rented with cash by a non-descript middle-aged man with a fake driver's license. When Euston joined me, we investigated the neighborhood but did not find anything helpful. I'm going over these old letters between Zilch and Enches." He ran his hands through the papers on his lap. "I'm hoping there's some clue about that list."

Rollie swallowed. "Cecily and I had an idea about where it could be." He quickly told Yardsly about the prowler in Zilch's vacant house.

Yardsly shrugged his narrow shoulders. "Euston believes the list does exist somewhere in London and that it is somewhat exposed. HOWEVER, Scotland Yard searched the house completely and found nothing of any significance. Still, it is peculiar that someone would return to the house. We've had the house under Scotland Yard surveillance since August. Just last week the surveillance team was reassigned to help look for the MUS list, so the house is now unguarded. Keep a wary eye out, lad."

"I wish there was some way I could help find that list or track Zilch. I feel useless."

Yardsly smiled. "I know you would do anything to help us. If I need you, I will not hesitate to contact you. In the meantime, enjoy your vacation."

Rollie nodded and left the office. He headed down the green carpeted hall to the end where the teachers' lounge was. Rollie found the oval table laden with pails, sponges, dusters, and cleaning detergents.

Eliot, with his shaggy raven hair and short pants, stood behind the cleaning supplies. "Rollie! It's about time!" he greeted in his usual blunt way.

Tibby and Margot, Cecily's two roommates, were giving Cecily hugs and swapping holiday stories. The other boy there was Rollie's other roommate Rupert. He was a tubby lad with brown hair and a round face. He was dressed in trousers and a gray sweater, and he wore plaid slippers. When he spotted Rollie, he brightened.

"Happy late Christmas," Rollie said. "How's your vacation been?"

Rupert shrugged. "Okay. I've been missing my roommates."

Rollie smiled. At first, he and Eliot had not gotten along with Rupert. Rupert had been envious of

Rollie's popularity, and Rollie had been suspicious of Rupert's mysterious behaviors. Rupert was an orphan who Yardsly had rescued off the streets, given a home to, and commissioned to be a Baker Street Irregular. Just as Holmes had, Yardsly hired orphans to be his messengers and errand runners. Recently, Rupert's duties as a Baker Street Irregular included helping with the investigation of MUS.

"Is everyone re-acquainted?" Eliot huffed. "We only have six hours!"

Everyone moaned.

"Six hours is barely enough time to clean this four-story building!" Eliot shrieked. "Let's assign jobs—"

"Headmaster wants me to clean the Rearranging Library," Rollie interrupted before Eliot got carried away.

"That's strange! Why?" Eliot narrowed his eyes.

"He has his reasons." Rollie shrugged casually.

Eliot shrugged back. "Fine, go ahead. I'll assign everyone else."

Grateful for an easy exit, Rollie grabbed a dusting rag and hurried back down the hall to Yardsly's office. The headmaster had stepped out, so Rollie helped himself to the little cupboard. He managed to carry all eight small marmalade jars and the rag in his arms. He carried them into the library off the hall.

In an armchair in the library sat Mr. Notch, the Observation teacher, with a newspaper spread across his knees. He chewed on the end of a pencil. He was dressed in his usual forest-green suit that was as wrinkled as ever. His bushy gray hair was in desperate need of a haircut, not to mention a little grooming.

"Oh, hello, Mr. Notch," Rollie said with some surprise.

"Well, hello, there . . . Rollin, is it?" Mr. Notch blinked his magnified eyes from behind very thick glasses. "Enjoying the holidays? What are you doing here?"

"We're doing Winter Cleaning, sir. Headmaster wants me to clean the library."

Mr. Notch peered at Rollie's armload of marmalade jars. "Oh!" He tapped his nose knowingly. "Let me just finish this last crossword clue, and I'll get out of your hair. Funny expression that—getting out of one's hair. I could very well see someone being trapped in *my* hair." He patted his unruly gray hair and gave a high-pitched laugh.

Rollie lined up the marmalade jars on the end table.

"Percy!" called a familiar voice from the hallway.

"In here, Amelia!"

Miss Hertz scurried into the library in search of her colleague. The short, plump woman sported equally unruly red hair streaked with a few grays.

"Hello, Print 20!" she squeaked at Rollie. "Very nice to see you. What have we here?" She lit up upon spotting the marmalade jars on the end table. "I *adore* glass jars! They always preserve the best fingerprints."

"Don't go interrupting him," Mr. Notch scolded. "Rollin has the very important task of cleaning the *library*." He tried to wink but could not quite coordinate it. He ended up blinking and twitching as if he had something in his eyes.

Miss Hertz nodded. "That is an important task to be sure. Percy, I locked myself out of my classroom and my keys are inside. Can you unlock it for me?"

Mr. Notch stood and folded his newspaper. He dug around in his pockets. "I seem to have misplaced my keys."

"Quite a pair we are!" Miss Hertz giggled. "Let's bother Yardsly. Happy cleaning, Print 20!"

The two absent-minded teachers exited the library.

Rollie closed the door, being careful to lock it as well. Flicking on the table lamp, he tried to get his bearings.

The small library boasted eight broad bookshelves crammed with all varieties of hardback books stacked atop each other. Every twenty-four hours, the shelves would automatically shuffle all the books around. In reality, this was just a distraction from the secret library hidden behind the shelves, which hid top-secret files on Academy students and alumni. In August, Rollie had discovered his marmalade jar from Auntie Ei was a key to opening the third shelf.

Rollie checked the bottom of the marmalade jars for their numbers engraved in the glass. He fitted the bottom of jar one into a small hole on the side of the first shelf. When he turned the jar with a click, the tall bookshelf yawned open. The secret shelves inside held students' Sherlock Holmes volumes labeled with their names.

Rollie did not dare open any of the books, for he knew they all contained private information on the students, such as addresses, IQ scores, family history, and medical records. He dusted and straightened the books, then closed the shelf with a click. He pulled out the jar, returned it to the table, and grabbed jar two. After cleaning the second shelf, he moved onto the third shelf. He was excited to clean this one because his volume was hidden there. He picked up the small marmalade jar and read the note from Auntie Ei still attached: *A good snack for the LIBRARY.*

By giving him this jar, Auntie Ei had helped him solve the case of the MUS burglar, who had turned out to be Professor Enches. Obviously, she had wanted him to succeed as a detective and help Sherlock Academy then. The idea that she didn't want him to be a student there anymore baffled him. There had to be more to that story . . .

He fit the jar in the hole and opened the shelf. The secret shelves inside were very untidy, for Enches had rummaged through the volumes when he had broken in last August. He had been searching for Rollie's volume.

Rollie dusted and straightened. He was about to close the shelf when he decided to take a look through his Sherlock Holmes volume, his favorite book. His records were pasted to the inside cover—all information he knew about himself. He flipped through the worn pages to his favorite Holmes case *The Adventure of the Empty House*, which he had bookmarked with his Holmes telegram. To his surprise, he

found several folded papers stuck between the pages.
He opened one and recognized the handwriting.

Sullivan,

*I know you have an interest in my great-nephew
Rollin, but I would rather he not attend the school under the circumstances we discussed earlier.*

Lady Wilson

Rollie gulped. So Yardsly was not the only person who had written a note about Rollie; Auntie Ei
had written back. He opened another letter with the
same monogram on the stationery.

Sullivan,

*By no means accept my great-nephew Rollin under
the circumstances we discussed. I do not wish him to
receive special privileges because of who I am and who
he will be.*

Lady Wilson

Rollie's middle fluttered. That elusive mention
of *circumstances* puzzled him. What were these mys-

terious circumstances that had made Auntie Ei not want Rollie to attend? And what had changed? He read the last letter.

Sullivan,

I appreciate your confidence in Rollin. It seems he shall be attending the Academy after all. However, I would prefer he be expelled rather than accepted under the circumstances. We shall watch and wait.

Lady Wilson

Rollie's heart raced. Auntie Ei had wanted him expelled? These *circumstances* must have been dire! He flipped through the rest of his volume in search of more letters. When he found none, he slid his book back into place.

He slid it out again. Quickly, he stuffed the unsettling letters into his pocket. He returned his book, closed the shelf, and set his marmalade jar on the end table.

His view of Auntie Ei started to tarnish. While she was privy to her own set of secrets, she was deliberately keeping secrets from him about *him*. He had always considered her his ally, for she had always wanted him to be a detective . . .

Or had she? It seemed at first she had not—under the *circumstances*.

Rollie needed to know the whole story, but now they were not even speaking to each other.

And for the first time, Rollie did not trust Auntie Ei.

Through the Window

"Thank you for helping with Winter Cleaning." Eliot was addressing the group now that they were gathered back in the teachers' lounge. "I consider this my first successful event as Student Government President. I hope I can count on you all again to help with future events."

"So what exactly are our positions in this government?" Wesley asked.

"Yes, are we automatically a part of it, or will there be elections?" Cecily chimed in.

Eliot cleared his throat unnecessarily loudly. "That is still to be determined. I would like to hold elections when we come back to school."

"Will your position be up for election?" Rollie asked.

"No, I already have my position as president."

"But we didn't vote for you," Tibby countered, polishing her little spectacles on her sweater.

"But I founded this Student Government, so I get to be president," Eliot said. "That's the rule. If you had founded it, you would be president."

Rupert gasped. "You're going to be president until you graduate from here? For the next three and a half years?"

"Sounds like a dictatorship to me." Margot shook her head of golden ringlets. "Not a proper form of government."

"It's not a dictatorship because other elected students will have a say in decisions," Eliot explained, his face heating. "Everyone will get to vote. I won't make all the decisions. That's how our Student Government works."

Wesley suppressed a mischievous grin. "So if the other students wanted to vote you out, they could."

"Well . . . yes," Eliot answered weakly.

Rollie patted Eliot on the back. "Don't worry, we won't vote you out. No one wants your position."

Eliot sighed with relief. "We're done here. Thanks again, chums."

Everyone turned to disband when a familiar face poked into the room.

"Fa-la-la, boys and girls!" a high voice sang.

"Lady Gram!" the girls cheered, rushing to give the petite teacher hugs.

Gwendolyn A. Gram stood barely a head taller than the children. Her blond curls were tied back with a red ribbon. She wore a holly-berry red velvet dress and matching high heels.

"I am so delighted to see you all!" she said, her blue eyes sparkling. "You saved me the task of addressing envelopes. I was just about to mail you the orchestra rehearsal schedule." She gave a sheet of paper to all the children except Rupert and Margot. "I assume you're still planning to be part of the orchestra."

The girls nodded eagerly, but the boys only shrugged.

"Tsk-tsk, gentlemen!" She wagged a scolding finger at them. "I'm counting on your attendance. We have a little over a month to rehearse for the Valentine concert. It's going to be a fundraiser for the school. I need everyone's help!"

"Speaking of which, Miss Gram," Eliot said, "as President of the Student Government, I would like to offer my help with the Valentine fundraiser."

"How very kind, Eliot! I will most definitely enlist your help with the fundraiser. We'll discuss it more when we come back from the holiday. Until then, I expect you all to attend rehearsal." Miss Gram sighed. "Mr. Chadwick will be here to help."

"We'll be here!" the boys said.

"Very well. I'll see you next week." She gave out another round of hugs to the girls then flitted away down the hall.

Cecily hugged Tibby and then Tibby mounted a hansom to return home. Cecily also bid good-bye to Margot who boarded at school fulltime since she was also a Baker Street Irregular. There was some debate about whether to split up and take two hansoms to the Wilson manor since hansoms held only two passengers, but Eliot argued that four children were the equivalent of two adults and they would fit fine. The children were cramped, but that kept them warm.

"I guess it's too late to explore the house," Wesley muttered.

"My dad might let us go," Rollie said. "He likes it when I do sleuth work."

"What are you talking about?" Eliot demanded.

The other three glanced at each other before Rollie caught Eliot up on the new mystery in Herr Zilch's vacant house.

"It's probably a hobo," Eliot said flippantly. "But it would be exciting to explore an empty house. Oh, did you read my secret note on the back of the letter I sent you?"

Rollie shook his head. "There was no note—it was blank."

Eliot rolled his eyes. "I wrote the message in invisible ink."

"How was I supposed to know that?"

"I figured you'd guess I used invisible ink when you saw it was blank."

"How do I reveal it? We haven't taken any chemistry classes."

Eliot narrowed his eyes at Rollie. "Are you serious? You really don't know?"

Rollie could not help scowling at his roommate. "Don't make me feel stupid!"

"I'm not! I'm just surprised—"

"Tell us how to reveal it!" Cecily snapped. "Right now!"

Rollie did not blame Cecily for being impatient with Eliot. Having endured a whole day of being bossed by Eliot, they were running low on patience with him.

"First of all, you know what to use to write invisibly, right?"

Rollie and Cecily shook their heads, but Wesley nodded.

"Think of the tools you got for your class schedule," he hinted.

"The pen!" Rollie shouted excitedly. "It writes with invisible ink? I never tried it."

"I tried to write with it but couldn't see anything," said Cecily. "I thought it had no ink."

Eliot grinned. "There's another tool. That pipe has the solution for invisible ink."

"Very clever!" Rollie exclaimed. "I can't wait to try it out." He glanced at the book Eliot held on his lap. "*The Bird Watcher's Guide for the English Moors.* You're into bird watching?"

"No. This cover is a decoy." Eliot slipped off the book jacket to reveal his textbook from school titled *On Secret Writings: One Hundred Sixty Separate Ciphers.* "I don't want to raise suspicion if any MUS agents see me reading this. These are dangerous times to be a detective."

The hansom stopped, the driver dismounted, and the children hopped out. They headed up the front walk and almost made it to the front door when a shower of snowballs pelted them from the front porch.

"Who threw that?" Eliot demanded with his hands on his hips.

Boisterous laughter was followed by the appearance of two lanky teenagers exchanging high-fives.

"Ed! Stew!" Rollie shouted.

Edward clapped his gloved hands together. "Just a little homecoming welcome."

"All in good fun!" Stewart added, tossing his scarf back over his shoulder.

"You won't get away that easily." Rollie scooped up snow, crunched it into a ball, and chucked it at his brothers. While Edward dodged it, Stewart was caught off guard. The snowball smacked him in the chest.

The boys tried to peg each other with snowballs while Cecily squealed and ducked out of their line of fire. Rollie threw a fast and well-aimed snowball at Edward again.

"Hey!" Edward hollered as the snowball exploded on his shoulder.

"Good one, Rollie!" Wesley said. "Forget rugby—you should play cricket. You've got a good bowl!"

After a few rounds of splattering each other with icy snowballs, the boys called a truce and everyone barged into the Wilson house. They stood in the entry hall dripping, panting, and laughing. While everyone else started stripping their outerwear, Edward and Stewart went in search of a pre-dinner snack.

"Fact: You all are having too much fun!" Mr. Wilson declared from the parlor.

He and Uncle Ky sat at a small card table by the fire. Atop the table, a jigsaw puzzle of an English landscape was taking form. The two men hunched over the puzzle, fitting different tiny pieces. Uncle Ky hummed a merry tune.

"I love puzzles!" Eliot crowed excitedly.

"You're welcome to join us," Mr. Wilson said.

"Who is this boy? I daresay, Peter, I can never keep track of all your children." Uncle Ky shook his head good humoredly. "I suppose you're making up for the lack of offspring from either Eileen or me. Do you have more stored in the basement, eh?"

Mr. Wilson chuckled. "This is Rollie's room-mate from school."

"I'm Eliot Simon Tildon."

"Well, Eliot Simon Tildon, are you any good at puzzles?" Uncle Ky snapped a puzzle piece into place.

"Dad, can we do a little sleuth work outside?" Rollie asked without hesitation. "Before supper?"

"Fact: Supper is in a half hour, so you had better hurry. Take your torches. There are some extra ones in the closet under the stairs."

The sleuths cheered. Everyone kept their winter garb on and got a flashlight. They headed back out into the frosty twilight. Their initial excitement gradually melted away to apprehension as they slushed through the snow toward Herr Zilch's dark mansion. Their laughter and loud voices lowered to whispers as they neared the front porch. They ducked under the black-and-yellow striped caution tape that roped off the porch, and mounted the steps. With their flashlights, they inspected the large padlocks on the front double-doors.

"The prowler did not use the front door," Wesley deduced. "How about the windows?"

Rollie and Eliot moved their beams along the window seams and tried to budge them. Cecily stood unusually close to Wesley.

"There must be another way in," Rollie whispered. "Around the back maybe."

"Should we be trespassing?" Cecily asked nervously.

The three boys looked at her and then each other.

Rollie shrugged. "No one lives here. We need to investigate, especially if there is a mystery involving

Herr Zilch. We need to for the good and safety of Sherlock Academy."

"You're right," said Cecily.

Wesley led the group to the right side of the house. The garden gate was not locked, so they easily entered the backyard. Another door stood on the back porch; it was also padlocked heavily. They continued along the back of the house, marching single-file through the snow behind Wesley, pointing their flashlights every which way.

"Hoot!" An owl flapped overhead.

Cecily yelped and gripped Wesley's arm. "Sorry, I'm a little scared, I have to admit."

"It's okay," Eliot assured her. "You're a girl."

"Excuse me?" Cecily snapped. "That is the dumbest rule you've ever made!"

"Shh!" Rollie tapped her. "Look down there."

They had reached the end of the house and stopped next to a window down by the ground.

"Does this house have a basement?" Wesley asked.

Rollie shrugged. "I guess. Ours does."

The three boys knelt in the snow and managed to pry open the window.

"We found the way in!" Wesley exclaimed. "I'll go first."

"I'll bring up the rear," offered Rollie. "Eliot, do you want to stand guard?"

"Absolutely not!"

"I'll stand guard," Wesley decided. "You guys need to find your way upstairs to open that drape."

Rollie, Cecily, and Eliot slipped through the window and dropped down to the ground inside the basement. They picked their way through several empty wooden crates.

Rollie led his comrades upstairs and into the kitchen, which was empty except for a cold black stove. The pantry shelves were bare and dusty, a few cobwebs running between them.

The house smelled old and musty, the air was frigid, and all the furniture was covered with white sheets. They stuck close together and warded off shadows with their bright beams. They found their way to the grand staircase. A crystal chandelier shrouded with cobwebs hung menacingly from the vaulted ceiling. Carefully, they mounted the marble stairs.

"This way," Rollie whispered, turning right down the hall on the second floor.

The dark-paneled walls displayed large paintings of various military commanders from the 1700s. They stood proudly, their hands resting on swords and their noses stuck up in the air. They all wore stern faces with cold eyes and seemed to judge the trespassers as they passed by.

Rollie poked his head into the first empty room but realized its window did not face his—it faced the street. At the end of the hall was a door. He led them there, poked his head in, and smiled. He crossed the room and pulled back the heavy drape. Through the window, he spotted his own bedroom window next door.

Click!

"No electricity," Eliot mumbled as he flicked the light switch up and down. "But there's this large lantern." He turned it on, bathing the room in a bright eerie glow.

"Eliot! Turn that off!" Cecily scolded.

"I thought we could get a better look around with the light on," Eliot said.

"We don't want anyone to see us in here!" Rollie stopped when he noticed brushes, trays, white sheets, and cans of paint in the center of the vacant room. "Is the prowler painting in here?" He touched the walls.

No fresh paint yet.

"That's odd!" Cecily commented. "The prowler's returned to paint the room?"

In the center of the room, the floorboards creaked and squeaked under their weight.

"We'd better get back home for supper. My mum doesn't like us to be late," Rollie said. He paused and sniffed. "What's that funny smell? It's not paint . . . "

The other two shrugged.

"There's not much to learn here," said Rollie. "We better head home."

After turning off the lantern, the sleuths hurriedly made their way back to the basement window where Wesley waited. He helped them exit up through it. Without a word, the group trudged back to the Wilson manor. Inside the entry hall, they pulled off their snow boots and wiggled out of their coats and scarves. They all felt a sense of security being back in the cheery warmth of the house. Rollie mentioned the strange paint supplies to Wesley.

"That *is* peculiar!" he agreed.

"The walls were not freshly painted though," Rollie said. "Maybe those supplies are old."

"No, I'll bet that's what we saw the prowler bringing in last night. Hopefully we'll know more tonight."

While his friends headed to the dining room for supper, Rollie took a moment to hide the letters he had snatched from the secret library at school. He raced upstairs to his room and stuffed the letters inside his hollow Shakespeare book he had brought home with him from school. In the hollow volume, he found his pen and pipe, both of which had been part of his class schedule back in August. He set those out on his desk to experiment with later.

He paused before going back downstairs.

Those letters puzzled him. On the one hand, he felt comforted knowing Headmaster Yardsly had advocated for Rollie to be his student. On the other hand, he felt alone without Auntie Ei's support right now. And it seemed he had never had it.

When he joined his family in the dining room, Rollie found them seated and digging into left over Christmas ham with all the trimmings. He avoided looking at Auntie Ei, though he could feel her piercing gaze on him. Due to all the guests staying with the Wilsons, another card table and four chairs had been set up in a corner of the dining room. This was reserved for Rollie and his three friends.

"Fact: We really have a full house now!" Mr. Wilson chuckled, nodding at the new guests. "Are you staying here, too, Cecily?"

Cecily shook her head of auburn curls. "I don't think there's room for me."

"You can stay in our room!" Lucille squealed.

"Yes! Please, Mummy, can she?" Daphne begged.

Mrs. Wilson smiled. "It's entirely up to Cecily if she wants to room with two chatty little girls."

Cecily and Rollie exchanged a knowing look.

Cecily shrugged. "I guess that could be fun. My parents are away visiting my Uncle Harry and Aunt Beryl in Manchester, and my brother doesn't like having to be in charge of me all the time."

Lucille and Daphne cheered, and proceeded to plan out the slumber party that would include making a tent and painting their toenails. Cecily dreaded the latter part of the plan, for she had never been much of a girly girl.

After dinner, Cecily went home to grab her pajamas and pillow. Eliot borrowed a sleeping bag from Stewart and set up camp next to Wesley on Rollie's limited floor space. Wesley checked the view into the now exposed room next door.

Rollie found Eliot's letter and flipped it over to the back. "How do I reveal the invisible ink?" he asked.

Eliot took the pipe and snapped off the mouthpiece. The end that had been attached to the pipe had a tiny brush. Inside the pipe bowl nestled a tiny bottle. He dipped the tiny brush into the tiny bottle, then stroked the brush across the paper. Soon, as if by magic, silvery words materialized.

P.S. Can I stay a few days longer with you?

"That's it? That's your secret message?" Rollie turned to Eliot. "Why did you write it in invisible ink?"

"In case bad guys intercepted your mail." Eliot nodded solemnly. "I didn't want them to know my plans." He snapped the mouthpiece back on the pipe bowl. "MUS agents could be anywhere!"

Rollie picked up the ballpoint pen. Underneath Eliot's postscript, he wrote *Yes, stay as long as you like.* At first, the ink looked shiny so he could see what he had written. Within a few seconds of exposed air, the ink dried into invisibility.

"Thanks," said Eliot after he revealed and read Rollie's response. "My father is busy moving my grandfather in to live with us."

"Is this the grandfather who gave you the Sherlock Holmes comic books?"

"He's the one. He's quite old and his health is failing, so Father thought it would be best if Grandfather lived with us in Edinburgh. I'm glad Father will have someone to keep him company while I'm away at school."

"Hallo, boys," Cecily said from the doorway. "Rollie, I got my notes from last summer. Maybe something I observed about Zilch and his secretary then will help us now." She thumped a worn notebook down on Rollie's desk. "You'll be sure to wake me up if anything happens next door, won't you? I'm not enslaving myself to your sisters for nothing."

"I'll wake you," Rollie promised as she left the room. "Don't worry."

The boys decided they were too excited to fall asleep, so they turned out the light and played rounds of Guess That Case. One boy would give clues and the others had to guess which Sherlock Holmes case he was referencing.

Eliot went first. "Dictionary, advertisement, red-hair—"

Wesley guessed first. "*The Case of the Red-Headed League!*"

"Okay," Wesley said. "Germans spies, kidnapping, factory—"

"*The Adventure of the Engineer's Thumb!*" Rollie and Eliot yelled at the same time.

"I got it first," Eliot decided.

"No you didn't! We got it at the same time," Rollie pointed out.

"I definitely heard my voice."

"Because you were louder!"

Wesley laughed. "You both got it at the same time. Besides, we're not keeping points."

"We're not?" Eliot gasped. "Then what's the point of this game?"

Rollie's bedroom door opened and a lanky figure stood in the doorway.

"Roly-poly, knock it off!" Edward hissed. "Stew and I have to go back to work tomorrow, which means we have to get up early, which means we have to get some sleep, which means you need to shut up!"

"Don't be such a grump, Ed," Rollie muttered.

"I'm warning you! Be quiet, or I'll make you!"

As Edward closed the door, the three boys buried their faces in their pillows and laughed.

Quietly, they continued playing Guess That Case until around two in the morning. Just when they were about to try another game, a light from outside cast shadows in Rollie's room. All three of them lunged for the window.

"Get Cecily!" Wesley whispered.

"I'm here!" she answered, joining them without warning. "I decided to check on you guys since I couldn't sleep."

They crowded together to peer out the window. The large lantern on the floor lit up the vacant room on the second floor. They could see the paint supplies in the middle of the room.

They waited and watched.

They stiffened when a figure marched into the room. The person was of average height and girth and was dressed all in black. A shock of long, brassy hair streaked from beneath a black knit cap.

"Is that who I think it is?" Rollie whispered.

Cecily squeezed his arm. "I think it's her!"

The prowler opened a can of white paint and poured a little into a paint tray. She dipped a wide brush into the paint and wiped it over the wall with a small fireplace.

"She's painting the room!" Wesley exclaimed. "Why?"

"Maybe she's a realtor fixing up the house to sell," Eliot suggested with a yawn.

"At two in the morning?" Rollie countered. "Besides, *she* is *not* a realtor."

For about fifteen minutes, they watched her paint the entire wall. She stood back to survey her work and catch her breath. She was about to dip her brush back in the paint tray when she froze.

Outside, a car rumbled by, screeched to a stop, and honked once.

The prowler hurriedly pressed the lid back on the paint can, set the brush in the tray, and turned off the lantern. She bolted out of the room.

"That must be her ride," Cecily deduced.

"So who is the prowler?" Wesley wanted to know.

Together, Rollie and Cecily said, "Herr Zilch's secretary!"

The Treasure in the Wall

The next morning the young detectives could barely get through breakfast, for they were too eager to explore Zilch's mansion. Finally, Mr. Wilson excused them from the table. First Eliot telephoned his father to say he was staying awhile longer with the Wilsons. Then they madly donned their winter garb and bolted outside. They went through Zilch's garden gate and over to the basement window. Finding it already open, they one by one dropped into the house. "There's some reason she painted this wall." Rollie crossed the room to the fireplace. "She must be on an important mission." When he touched the wall it felt cold and damp.

"And so far, she's painted only this wall," added Wesley. "Do you think she's going to return to paint the rest of the room?"

"What was this room anyway?" Cecily wondered. "A bedroom?"

"It was an office," Eliot stated plainly. When the others looked at him in surprise, he explained, "It has no closet, only one window, a fireplace, and it's rather small compared to the other rooms here. I doubt it's a bedroom. It must have been Herr Zilch's study."

"Good deduction," Wesley said. "His study would be the most important room in the house. His secrets would have been kept here."

"There must be a secret still here if the secretary's returned," Rollie muttered.

"There doesn't seem to be much more we can learn from this room. Maybe we should explore the rest of the house," Wesley suggested. He headed back into the hall, the others following.

They avoided eye contact with the militant portraits as they ventured down the hallway. Rollie poked into the first door on the right. He flicked on the light switch, but no light went on. By the gloomy glare from the window, he could tell the room was bare. Eliot said the same about the room across from it.

"I don't see anything interesting." Eliot yawned. "I'm bored."

"Let's play a good ol' game of hide-and-seek!" Wesley suggested with a mischievous glimmer in his brown eyes.

"This house is perfect for a hiding game," Rollie agreed. "Not it!"

"Not it!" Wesley and Cecily yelled.

"That's not fair!" protested Eliot. "I didn't know it was time for that. It's time now—not it!"

"*You're* not fair," Rollie pointed out.

"I'll be it," Wesley consented. "This dead end of the hall is safe. I'll count to fifty. Go!"

The others scattered as Wesley faced the wall, closed his eyes, and started counting.

Rollie knew exactly where to hide. He raced to the largest bedroom, which he guessed was the master suite. The large fireplace still had a black iron heat screen. Scooting the fireguard aside, Rollie crawled into the fireplace and dragged the screen back into place. Having held no fire for months, the fireplace was fairly clean.

He found himself wondering if this room had been where Herr Zilch had slept. Since it was the largest bedroom, it had probably been his sanctuary. He tried to imagine Herr Zilch sleeping in a large bed, opening the drapes each morning, reading the morning paper in front of a roaring fire . . .

But it was hard to imagine the criminal mas-
termind doing normal things that other people did.
Still, being in Zilch's bedroom did make him a little
more human in Rollie's mind.

"Ready or not, here I come!" Wesley's voice sounded faintly from down the hallway.

Rollie leaned into the corner.

Scra-a-a-p-e!

Rollie jerked in surprise—the bricks beneath his
head budged. He turned around and rested his palm
where his head had been leaning against the fireplace.
Two bricks were loose. He pulled them out of place.
A dark space about a foot wide and a foot high was
carved into the fireplace. He was about to stick his
hand into the space when he remembered his fellow
detectives. Instead he kicked the heat shield aside
and scrambled out of his hiding spot. He rushed into
the hallway just as Cecily flew by, Wesley close on
her heels.

Wesley skidded to a stop to tag Rollie.

"I found something!" Rollie yelled excitedly.

"You're it!" Wesley grinned. "Cecily and Eliot
are safe."

"Never mind the game—"

"I was just getting into it!" Eliot whined.

"Come see what I found." Rollie led his friends back into the master bedroom and over to the fireplace. "I think it's a secret—"

"A secret passage?" Cecily blurted.

"Like at school?" Wesley nodded knowingly.

"There's a secret passage at school?" Eliot shrieked.

The others grimaced. Eliot was not supposed to know about that.

Rollie pointed out the dark hole in the fireplace.

"Do you think there's something in there?" Cecily asked, hoping to divert Eliot's attention.

"There's a secret passage at school?" Eliot pressed. "How come I didn't know about it?"

"We'll explain later," said Rollie. "There might be something hidden in there." He reached his hand toward the space when Cecily snatched it aside.

"Don't stick your hand in there!" she gasped. "There could be anything in there—like spiders or snakes!"

"It could be a trap. This *is* the enemy's house. We need a torch." Wesley straightened up. "Should I go get one from your room, Rollie?"

"I'll go with you," Cecily offered.

Wesley and Cecily hurried off, while Rollie and Eliot plopped down on the carpet beside the fireplace to wait.

"Tell me about this secret passage at school," Eliot demanded.

"I guess I have no choice now." Reluctantly, Rollie explained there was a secret passage that ran inside the walls of the Academy on all four floors. There was a secret entrance on each floor and also one to the outside alley. He did not mention the Sherlockian antiques stored on the third floor.

Following this explanation, Eliot peppered Rollie with more questions, mostly about why no one else knew about it and why his friends *did* know about it. He went on to argue it was unfair that some students knew about this Academy secret while others were in the dark. He thought this gave others an unfair advantage. He begged Rollie to show him where the secret openings were, but Rollie refused without Headmaster's Yardsly's permission. Eliot then said he was entitled to the secret passage since he was the Student Government President, no less. He decided to write up a demand to Yardsly for secret passage access.

Rollie told him not to.

Eliot said he would anyway.

Rollie wanted to smack Eliot.

Finally, Wesley and Cecily returned with a flashlight.

Wesley shined the flashlight into the small, dark hole. "There is something in there—it doesn't look like a spider or a snake." He elbowed Cecily playfully.

Rollie stuck his hand fearlessly into the cache. His fingers felt something smooth and dusty. He pulled out a leather-bound book of some kind. He blew off the coat of dust and trailing cobwebs from the book.

Cecily sneezed.

"Bless you," said Wesley.

She blushed. "Thank you."

Rollie opened the book and read the first page. "*Property of F. A. Zilch.* This is Herr Zilch's journal!" He flipped through the worn pages of handwritten notes.

"He kept a journal?" Wesley peered closer at the pages. "Of what? His dastardly deeds as the MUS leader?"

Rollie read the first entry aloud. "24 May 1921: Today marks the one-month anniversary of my sister's death. It also marks the day I have been granted guardianship of her son. Her daughter, my niece, is of age to be independent; she is attending Oxford. My nephew is a quiet boy but intelligent nonetheless. I never thought I would have a child to look after, but I am obligated to take charge of him. My sister's death grieves me so, but my nephew's presence helps to alleviate my grief. I hope he enjoys living in London."

"Zilch told you about his nephew once, didn't he, Rollie?" Cecily questioned. "Didn't he mention that his nephew had attended Sherlock Academy long ago?"

Rollie nodded. "I should ask Headmaster about him sometime."

"We didn't know Zilch's sister died and he was his nephew's guardian," added Cecily.

"Poor Zilch," Eliot said quietly.

The other three gaped at him.

"Poor Zilch!" Wesley growled. "He will never have my pity, not after all he's done to us . . . to me." He rubbed the bruise on his forehead.

"Anyone who has lost a loved one should have pity," Eliot lectured in a sad tone. "I know what it's like to lose someone you love. My mum."

Wesley's face softened. "What happened to your mum?"

"She died," Eliot said bluntly. "Cancer—I don't remember what kind. I just remember being worried and sad, and then one day she was gone. I was four."

Everyone placed a sympathetic hand on Eliot's shoulders.

He smiled. "I'm fine now, so don't feel too sorry for me. It's just the way my life turned out to be. And I'll say it again: poor Zilch."

"And poor nephew," Cecily whispered. "Does the journal mention his name?"

"Let's take this home and read more." Rollie closed the journal and tucked it under his arm. He replaced the loose bricks in the hole inside the fireplace and readjusted the screen.

As he and his friends made their way back to his house, Rollie thought about Herr Zilch. He was curious to know more about the villain by reading the journal. He knew it was hard having a loved one die. He had not experienced that yet, but the thought of losing someone he loved, like a family member or friend, made him sad. Even if he was a criminal, Herr Zilch had been sad to lose his sister.

Maybe there was another side to Herr Zilch, just as there seemed to be another side to Auntie Ei.

A side Rollie had never considered.

Herr Zilch's Story

The sleuths gathered before the parlor fireplace to take the cold out of their bones. Mrs. Wilson brought them hot chocolate to help with the chill. Once they were all cozy on the warm carpet, Rollie opened Herr Zilch's journal and flipped to the second entry.

"5 June 1921: This morning I was summoned to Glasgow. The director of MUS headquarters there has been missing for a fortnight. I fear he may have been captured. I was reluctant to leave Nephew. He is still in mourning for his mother. Her death has been quite a blow to him, especially since he mysteriously lost his father only a few years ago. His father, a government agent, has been missing in action and is assumed dead. My niece is traveling abroad this summer and has no desire to be with family. Perhaps it is her way of coping. As for Nephew, I have not told him of my work, but I would not doubt he has formed his own suspicions of me."

"Glasgow!" Eliot exclaimed. "That's in Scotland—I live in Scotland! I wonder if that MUS branch is still there. Or if there are any in Edinburgh where I live."

"We should turn this journal over to Headmaster," Rollie decided. "It could help him find Herr Zilch."

"Good idea." Cecily sipped her hot chocolate. "But not until we've read the whole thing. We need every clue we can get to help us right now, too."

Rollie flipped to the third entry. "28 June 1921: My worst fear has been realized. While I was away on MUS business, Nephew received an invitation to attend a brand new detective school: Sherlock Academy of Fine Sleuths. I am not sure how they found him. The invitation was sent to his postal box in town, which is a relief. If they were to find him living with me, my cover could be exposed. As of now, there is no possible way for anyone associated with the Academy to connect me to Nephew since our last names are different.

"30 June 1921: I have tried dissuading Nephew from attending Sherlock Academy. That is the last thing I want for him. However, he is most intrigued, and it seems my dissuasions are only making him more interested. I have no choice but to allow him to attend orientation tomorrow, being the first of July.

"7 July 1921: Nephew has been accepted to the Academy. This does not entirely surprise me, for I knew he was an intelligent lad. At first I was livid, but I have come to realize that this could be a benefit in disguise. I can use Nephew as a spy inside the Academy—"

"So I wasn't the first kid he used," Wesley interrupted bitterly.

"—to learn its weaknesses. If he is intelligent enough for Sherlock Academy, he is intelligent enough for MUS. I have made it my personal mission to destroy Sherlock Academy, for I cannot allow scores of Sherlockian detectives to interfere with MUS. Furthermore, this vendetta holds personal significance to me, for the headmaster is none other than my former colleague Sullivan Yardsly." Rollie paused to voice his own thoughts. "Yardsly and Zilch were colleagues?"

"How? When?" Eliot shot off. "Read!"

"13 August 1921: I have been extremely preoccupied with MUS affairs, so I have not had a moment to make an entry. But this week's catastrophe merits recording. I harbored hopes of using Nephew as a spy inside Sherlock Academy. I made the assumption he would want to help his uncle and guardian. I decided it was time to tell him about my work with MUS and my desire to destroy the Academy. I related the history of MUS, dating back to Professor Moriarty himself. I explained how my hard work and cunning had earned me leadership of the entire society. I also told him I wanted to name him heir to my position. He was quite stunned, but he said he would take some time to consider everything before giving me an answer. I shared my deepest fear with him: I fear being defeated by another great detective just as Moriarty was defeated by the great detective Holmes. I must close Sherlock Academy to keep the school from producing such a detective!"

"That makes sense," Cecily interjected. "Rollie! That's why he's taken an interest in you! He's afraid you could be that great detective to stop him someday."

Everyone was silent as Cecily's observation registered.

Auntie Ei's words from October echoed in Rollie's memory: *There is a reason you were chosen to attend*

105

Sherlock Academy. Headmaster Yardsly knows it, I know it, and Herr Zilch knows it."

He still wondered about the reason he was chosen. Was it based merely on his promising abilities as a detective? Was Yardsly hoping he would one day be the great detective to defeat Herr Zilch once and for all, just as Holmes had defeated Moriarty?

In opposition, did Auntie Ei not think Rollie could defeat Zilch? There were *circumstances* that made her hesitate allowing him to attend Sherlock Academy. Had she thought he would not be good enough?

Flutter, flutter! went his middle.

Wesley nudged Rollie. "Are you alright, mate?"

Rollie swallowed. "I'll bet he fears you, Wesley. That's the reason he tricked you into being his spy. You're a promising detective, too."

Wesley smiled. "Thanks, mate, but I think Cecily is right about you being the ultimate threat."

Rollie turned a page in the journal. "17 August 1921: I am undone! My attempt at honesty with Nephew has backfired. He has betrayed me. He has told Yardsly everything: that I am his uncle, that I want him to be my spy, and that I want him to inherit my position as leader of MUS. He has even told Yardsly where we are living. It seems Nephew has been brainwashed by the Academy's doctrine. I feared this. I have no choice but to leave our West End flat and go underground for a while. I must disown Nephew. When I feel it is safe, I will search for a new residence, perhaps in a quiet suburb. While my first priority is and will always be MUS, I hate to confess . . . I am heartbroken."

"That's not how I expected the story to turn out," Wesley admitted. "I assumed the nephew betrayed Sherlock Academy by taking Zilch up on his offer to be the MUS spy."

"Me too!" Rollie closed the journal. "But this nephew turned out to be a good guy."

"Is there more in the journal?" Cecily wanted to know.

"The whole journal is full. It will take us awhile to read through the whole thing." Rollie set the journal down on the carpet and took a sip of cocoa, which had cooled considerably. "I wouldn't be surprised if there are clues and codes hidden in his journal. Maybe that's why this journal was hidden away in that secret hole."

"I'm surprised Zilch didn't take this journal with him when he fled the house," said Wesley.

"He probably forgot all about it," replied Rollie as he flipped to the last page. "His last entry was in 1927—that was a while ago. It was hidden in the fireplace, and he left in a great hurry."

"Now do you feel pity for him?" Eliot blurted. "He lost his sister and his nephew all in one year. One to death and one to betrayal—I don't know which is worse."

"I can't say because I've never lost anyone to death," Rollie muttered. "But I have been betrayed, and it was the worst feeling in the world." He glanced at Wesley, whose brow furrowed with regret.

"This nephew must have been quite brave to betray his uncle," Eliot said quietly. "Uncle Zilch was his only family left besides his sister. I don't know if I could ever be that brave. I don't have a lot of family either—just my father, my grandfather, and one aunt. I'd have a hard time betraying any of them."

"Maybe you wouldn't if they were bad guys like Zilch," Rollie countered. "But you're right: this nephew was very brave."

Eliot sighed. "I wish we knew more about him or knew who he was."

"I've been thinking," began Cecily. "We're sort of a team now—the four of us. Don't you think we should make our team official? We should name ourselves."

"Yes! A great name," Eliot agreed, getting excited. "Like the Anti-Moriarty Underground Society."

Cecily wrinkled her nose. "Too long."

"The Four Sleuths."

"Too short!"

"We need to give this some serious thought," Wesley agreed. "It's only right to include Holmes in our name."

"I agree." Rollie fingered the leather journal. "We've become a team mainly to stop Zilch and fight MUS. We need a strong name. Wesley, what was the name of Euston's club?"

"The Holmes Brigade!"

"Let's use that name—it's great!" Rollie decided. "Watch out, MUS!"

"Euston's in a secret club?" asked Cecily.

Wesley nodded. "He wears a leather wristband with a strange symbol on it. He's part of the Holmes Brigade. That's all I know. I wish we could ask him more about it."

The new Holmes Brigade made deductions about the present mystery of Zilch's whereabouts, the nephew's identity, and the secretary's strange painting. They wanted to spend the afternoon reading the rest of the journal, but their sleuth work was interrupted. Mrs. Wilson had a task for them.

"Tomorrow is New Year's Eve," she announced, collecting their empty mugs. "Daddy thinks we should host a little party, mainly to keep Edward and Stewart out of trouble because they've been invited to a few parties. Is everyone up for that?"

They gave their hearty consent.

"Would you mind coming up with some games or activities for the evening?" Mrs. Wilson looked from one detective to the other. "Of course, we'll do a midnight countdown and have party crackers to pop. It would be fun to have some games to play before then."

"Sure, Mum, we'll come up with something," Rollie told her.

"Great. Please include your sisters. Lucille! Daphne!" Mrs. Wilson left the parlor as the twin girls came running in.

Lucille plopped onto the carpet next to Eliot. Daphne flanked his other side and stared at him with dreamy blue eyes. Eliot looked a little uncertain of this attention. He scooted closer to Rollie.

Wesley suggested they create some Sherlockian games like pin the pipe on Holmes. Cecily came up with Sherlockian charades and Pictionary.

"How about a kissing game?" Lucille managed to say between giggles.

Daphne giggled uncontrollably at her sister's suggestion.

"Ew! What's wrong with you, Lu?" Rollie scrunched his nose in disgust.

"It's New Year's Eve," Lucille reasoned. "Everyone will kiss someone at midnight. We could make a game out of it."

"I know who I'm going to kiss," Daphne said softly, casting a shy look at Eliot.

"You can't kiss anyone," Rollie said sternly. "You're seven. Only Mum and Dad get to kiss each other. Oh, and Ed and Stew will kiss their girlfriends."

"Not on the lips!" Lucille gagged. "We can't do that, but we can peck 'em on the cheek. Who are you going to kiss, Cecily?"

Cecily blushed slightly. "I don't need a kiss from a boy."

"If no one kisses you, I'll give you a peck on the cheek," Lucille promised.

"Thank you." Cecily smiled. After a moment's pause, she turned to Wesley. "Do you have a girlfriend?"

Wesley laughed. "No—but I did like Hazel at school."

"The tall girl?" Cecily narrowed her eyes. "She's on the fencing team."

"Yeah, but I think she likes my friend Todd."

Rollie rolled his eyes. "Let's get back to planning New Year's Eve."

Mrs. Wilson gave Wesley a sheet of butcher paper to draw a large Holmes silhouette on. She also gave him extra drawing paper for the pipes and scissors to cut them out. While Wesley worked on his Holmes silhouette, Eliot drew and cut out the pipes. Rollie and Cecily wrote prompts on little squares of paper for charades and Pictionary. They sat side by side on the sofa.

"Rollie," Cecily elbowed him. "I hope I didn't scare you with what I said about Herr Zilch fearing you. About you being the great detective to stop him."

Rollie cocked his head to one side. "Honestly, it does scare me a little, but I already knew Zilch had an interest in me. That alone is scary. He's been trying his hardest to get me to back off."

"You shouldn't worry about it," Cecily said. "You're a good detective now, and you'll only get better. Headmaster and Auntie Ei believe in you, and they'll always help you out. So will I."

"Thanks, Cecily." He wrote another prompt on a slip of paper. "I'm not so sure about Auntie Ei anymore." Lowering his voice, he told her about the letters he had found at school. He shared his confusion over Auntie Ei's initial reluctance to have him attend Sherlock Academy and how he distrusted her at the moment.

"That makes no sense!" Cecily exclaimed. Remembering to be hushed, she added in a lower tone, "Maybe those circumstances have to do with Herr Zilch. Maybe Auntie Ei knew Zilch was gunning for you and wanted to protect you from him."

"But that still doesn't explain why she lets me attend the Academy now. It doesn't explain why she gave me the marmalade jar and the newspaper map—both helped me stop Herr Zilch. In October, she told me never to stop looking out for Zilch. I thought she wanted me to help stop him."

Cecily shook her head of auburn curls. "I don't know, Rollie. You should just talk to her about it."

Rollie grunted. "We're not speaking to each other right now. I don't want to get into it. The important thing is figuring out why Zilch's secretary painted that wall last night."

"Yes, we mustn't lose sight of the real case here. Let's watch out for her tonight. I'll spend the night again. My parents will be away until next week."

"I wonder if the secretary will finish painting the study . . . and why in the world she is doing it."

Auld Lang Syne

They were disappointed; Zilch's secretary did not return that night.

After exploring the vacant house more and finding nothing of interest the next morning, they built snow forts in the Wilson's back garden for a while. Then when Cecily mentioned her interest in trying out for the fencing team next year, Wesley offered to coach her. He found two sticks about the size of fencing foils and marked a practice area in the snow. Cecily caught on quickly, much to Wesley's surprise and delight. When the temperature dropped and the daylight faded in the late afternoon, they joined the rest of the Wilson family indoors to prepare for the New Year's Eve party.

Wesley tacked the large Holmes silhouette on a blank wall in the parlor. Rollie tacked some more butcher paper beside the Holmes silhouette for Pictionary. Cecily and Eliot moved around the furniture to allow room for acting out charades. Edward and Stewart blew up a plethora of different colored balloons. Mrs. Wilson set out glass bowls of popcorn and candy. Mr. Wilson brought out boxes of party crackers while Lucille and Daphne hunted around the aging Christmas decorations for mistletoe. Uncle Ky stood back, his hands jingling coins in his pockets, and watched all the bustle with amusement. Auntie Ei stayed away until the last minute.

Around eight o'clock, a few neighborhood friends, including the teen twins' girlfriends, arrived to join the party. Once Auntie Ei came out of hiding, Mr. Wilson organized the first round of Pin the Pipe on Sherlock. Each contestant took a turn wearing a blindfold and pinning a pipe as close to Holmes' mouth as possible. Everyone was fairly off base, pinning pipes on Holmes' shoulders and arms and head. Edward came the closest. While they played, Uncle Ky sat in an armchair, occasionally nodding off.

Next, everyone played Sherlockian charades. Mr. Wilson proved quite goofy with his actions, making everyone, except Auntie Ei, laugh heartily. The game was going along fine when something unusual happened.

Auntie Ei finally laughed.

Now for all who knew her well, they remembered only two actual laughs from the elderly woman. The first laugh on record happened when Rollie was a toddler. He had mimicked Auntie Ei's favorite Holmes saying, "Elementary, my dear Watson!" His little voice and cute appearance coupled with the ridiculous notion of a toddler saying this phrase had compelled a hearty laugh out of Auntie Ei. The second instance was when Edward's experiment with a new edgy haircut went awry. Auntie Ei had bust out in laughter, which was a little mocking but well deserved.

Now for the third time, Auntie Ei chuckled aloud. She apparently found Eliot's impersonation of a bloodhound on the trail rather amusing. He scampered on his hands and knees, his nose pressed to the carpet. He wore such an earnest expression, and his shaggy hair flopped about so like a dog, that he caused everyone to laugh, including Auntie Ei.

Watching Auntie Ei laugh almost made Rollie forget about their fight. When he remembered it, he regretted it. He wanted to make amends with her just so life would not be awkward together. But there were some things he needed to sort out, one being whether he still trusted her.

"We've got five minutes to go!" Mr. Wilson announced as he read his pocket watch. "Fact: Then it will be a new year!"

When it was finally time, the group shouted the countdown together: "Ten, nine, eight . . . "

Rollie noticed Cecily standing next to Wesley by the fire. He joined them.

" . . . five, four, three, two, ONE! Happy New Year!"

A commotion erupted not only in the Wilson house but also out in the neighborhood as everyone rang in the New Year. Mr. and Mrs. Wilson shared a tender kiss. Stewart shyly kissed his girlfriend, Alice, on the cheek. She blushed. Edward boldly kissed his girlfriend, Beth, on the lips—she slapped him back with a blush and a giggle. Wesley and Cecily stood by each other, awkwardly shuffling their feet.

"Rollie, tell your sisters to leave me alone!" Eliot begged as he cowered behind Rollie. "They keep trying to kiss me!"

"Hey, stop that, Lu and Daph!" Rollie scolded. "I'll tell Dad what you're trying to do."

With giggles, Lucille and Daphne backed off.

"Time for crackers!" Mr. Wilson announced, passing the box around.

According to British tradition, crackers were a part of almost any festivity. Crackers were a tube wrapped in colorful foil-like paper. Two people pulled on either end and the cracker tore in two with a crack or pop. One person would get the bigger half and thus get the special prize and fortune inside.

Rollie grabbed a yellow one and immediately turned to Cecily. "Be my partner?"

Cecily's green eyes snapped from Rollie to Wesley and back. "Oh, uh, I was going to be Wesley's partner."

"I need a partner," said Eliot.

Rollie turned to Eliot. Each boy gripped the end of the cracker with his fingers. On three, they both pulled. The cracker split with a pop, confetti sprinkled the carpet, and Eliot was left with the bigger piece. He pulled out a paper crown and placed it proudly on his head. Then he read his fortune aloud.

"*You will find success in all your endeavors.* Crikey!" Eliot beamed. "Perhaps this means I'll solve the prowler mystery."

"Shh!" Rollie cautioned with a nervous glance at Auntie Ei; luckily, her attention was focused on her brother.

Uncle Ky treated the family to a little singing. In a clear tenor voice, he sang *Auld Lang Syne*. The family applauded when he was finished, and he gave a little bow.

As the night grew older, the neighbors and girl-friends headed home. Mrs. Wilson told the family not to clean up the party mess until tomorrow. They headed upstairs to get ready for bed. Cecily was invited to stay again since her older teenage brother was out partying. He thought his parents' absence gave him permission to do so; Cecily said she knew he would pay for his rowdy escapades when their parents returned next week.

The Wilson household slept in until around ten the next morning. Rollie was the first to wake while his roommates slumbered on. His tummy growled with hunger, so he wrapped himself in his robe and slipped downstairs. In the dining room, he found Uncle Ky sipping his morning tea, reading the *Daily Telegraph* newspaper, and humming a tune.

"Oh, good morning, Rollin, and happy New Year. Have some tea?"

Rollie poured himself a cup of tea and sat down at the long, empty table.

"So, Rollin, how are you enjoying school—at the Academy, that is?"

"I love it. It's a lot of work, but I love my teachers and everything I'm learning."

"Good, good. Being happy—that's important, you know."

"Have you ever been to Sherlock Academy, Uncle Ky?"

Uncle Ky folded the newspaper. "I believe I have. When was it? Oh, yes, when it first opened—how many years ago was it? Ten years ago, I think. I attended the opening ceremony that Eileen hosted."

"She hosted a ceremony? I wasn't sure when she got involved with the school."

"Oh, yes, she's been involved since the beginning—even before, I suppose. She wanted me to be involved too, but I knew it wasn't for me. I knew I would just end up letting her down later on, you know."

"I think you're swell to do what you want and not care what other people think."

"Thank you, Rollin, that's very kind of you to say so. I never considered myself *swell*, as you put it, but

I suppose I am, now that you mention it. I've learned not to let others define who I am. I define myself."

Rollie sipped his tea and thought about this. "Sherlock Holmes believed that, too. He never let other people's opinions stop him from being who he was. And there were a lot of people who thought his methods were a little crazy."

Uncle Ky nodded. "You are correct. He defined himself as a detective, Mr. Holmes did. Because he defined himself, he was the best! I have a feeling you are a lot like Mr. Holmes, eh?"

Rollie smiled. "I hope to be, but I do care a little what other people think of me. I care a lot about what Auntie Ei thinks of me. Right now we're in a fight though."

"I noticed you were not as chummy with each other as you usually are. Don't worry, ol' boy, you'll make up. She's not as crusty as she seems on the out-side." He winked.

"I know." Rollie sighed. "I just don't like when she keeps secrets from me."

"Ah, yes, she does like her secrets, that sister of mine." Uncle Ky leaned his elbows on the table. "I know some of her secrets, you know."

Rollie's eyes widened. "About me?"

"Perhaps. I know a secret about your lineage."

"Really? She mentioned my lineage a while ago, but she won't tell me anything else about it."

"Well, there's nothing you can do about it until you are of age. Seventeen, I think, but I could be wrong—"

"Good morning, gentlemen." Auntie Ei entered the dining room, eyed Rollie, then sat down next to Uncle Ky, and poured herself a cup of tea. "You seem to be engaged in an interesting conversation."

Uncle Ky winked at Rollie. "Yes, indeed, we were discussing New Year's resolutions. Do you have any, Eileen?"

"I never make resolutions—I make goals."

"What's the difference?" asked Rollie.

Auntie Ei glanced at him. "A resolution is wishful thinking; a goal is an intentional plan. I am very intentional, therefore I make goals, not resolutions."

"Maybe your goal this year should be to keep fewer secrets," Rollie mumbled.

"And your goal should be to cease this nosey behavior and to stop ransacking a certain relative's bedroom!" Auntie Ei shot back.

"My goal is to win at least one more singing competition," Uncle Ky added. He cleared his throat and launched into a song.

"Stop it this instant!" Auntie Ei snapped. "I have a headache."

Rollie sighed in exasperation. Leaving his tea behind, he stormed out of the dining room. As he climbed upstairs, he calmed down. So far he did not like how this new year was starting out.

He did not like Auntie Ei's keeping secrets about him. He did not like those letters that seemed to indicate she was not his avid supporter the way he had thought she was. Yet she was right about him searching her bedroom. It was a breach of the etiquette and respect between them. Rollie did feel sorry for doing it.

He also did not like not knowing what Herr Zilch's secretary was up to by painting that wall in the vacant house. Uncle Ky and his encouragement were the only redeeming things about the day so far. When he entered his room, he found one more thing he did not like.

"Eliot, why are you messing up my books?"

Eliot sat on the floor by the bookcase. He had emptied the shelves and was rearranging the books. "I'm arranging your books the way they should be arranged: in alphabetical order by author's last name, just like any respectable library."

"See the labels on the shelves? That's how I arrange my books."

Eliot shook his head. "This rating system is too subjective to your opinions! That's no way to arrange a bookcase. The rule is in alphabetical order by—"

"Fine! Do whatever you want with my books." Rollie threw himself into the chair at his desk.

"Well, you're in a fine mood," Eliot mumbled sarcastically. "Don't get too peevish with me. It was your Aunt Eileen's suggestion I reorganize your bookshelves."

"What!" yelled Rollie, his face heating.

"She brought it to my attention and suggested I right it." Eliot slid a few books into place on the top shelf. "And I'm very glad she did, though I would have noticed this disarray sooner or later."

"She only suggested it to get back at me," mumbled Rollie.

Wesley stretched in his sleeping bag. "Are you alright, mate?" he asked with a yawn.

"I'm frustrated," muttered Rollie.

"About this mystery next door?"

"Yes, and more." Rollie peered through his binoculars and out the window.

"I'm sure Zilch's secretary will show up again." Wesley pulled on his robe. "We'll figure this out. In the meantime, I need to do more homework."

"Rise and shine, sleepy-heads!" Mrs. Wilson sang through the hall. She was greeted with moans and groans from the rest of the sleeping family. "It's New Year's Day and you know what that means!"

"What does that mean?" Eliot asked excitedly. He had grown to expect great things from the Wilsons.

"It means we have to take down all the Christmas decorations and pack them away in the basement," Rollie said without enthusiasm. "It's not that fun."

"Anything is fun with your family," Eliot said. "I haven't had this much fun in a long time. I think I'll spend the holidays with you every year if you don't mind."

"Count me in too." Wesley beamed. "I only have one sibling, so hanging out with this lot is great fun."

Rollie got dressed and led his friends down to breakfast. Silently, he ate his hash browns and avoided looking at Auntie Ei. He hated being in this foul mood, especially on New Year's Day, but at the moment there were too many things weighing on him.

And he decided he hated secrets.

Mr. Chad's Clue

"**S**he's back!" Rollie whispered, rousing his friends just after midnight. It had been four days since the secretary's last return to the mansion.

Everyone, including Cecily, crowded around his window. Through it, they spotted Zilch's secretary surveying the walls in the study next door. Since the drape was still open, they had a clear view of her. She again wore a long, black coat and black knit cap. Her brassy hair trailed down her back.

"Is she going to paint more?" Cecily wondered quietly.

"The paint supplies are still there," Wesley noted.

"Why is she painting one wall at a time?" asked Eliot. "What a waste of time! Just do it all at once."

"She ran out of time before," Rollie replied. "I bet tonight she'll finish the room."

They watched her grab the paintbrush, dip it in the can of paint she had just opened, and turn back to the wall. It took her about fifteen minutes to paint the wall. Just as she was painting around the window, she paused. Suddenly, she peered out.

"She sees us!" Rollie hissed, dropping to the floor.

Everyone else hit the floor also. They lay on their sides and breathed heavily, full of anxiety and the fear of being spotted. The light from next door dimmed then went off completely.

Cautiously, Rollie eased up and peeked over the top of his desk. "She's gone and she closed the drape."

The others scrambled up.

"I'm sure she saw us," murmured Cecily.

"She knows we know," Wesley whispered solemnly. "This is serious."

"What can she do to us?" Eliot replied flippantly.

The other three locked eyes with him.

"It's not what she'll do, it's what Herr Zilch will do," said Rollie.

Eliot's dark eyes widened with fear. "What will he do? How can we be safe? Should we tell your parents?"

"Shh!" Rollie cautioned. "No, we'll tell Headmaster Yardsly when we go to school for orchestra rehearsal tomorrow."

Without another word, Cecily returned to Lucille and Daphne's bedroom, and the boys scrambled back under their covers. While they lingered awake for a while, they did not speak to each other. They did not need to; they were all thinking the same thing . . .

. . . Herr Zilch knew they knew.

* * * *

Knock-knock!

"COME IN!"

The young sleuths entered Headmaster Yardsly's office. They had arrived at Sherlock Academy a few minutes before orchestra rehearsal to talk with their headmaster, and they were relieved to find him in.

Yardsly stood behind his large, cluttered desk. He was dressed in a charcoal-gray suit and a red tie. In one hand he held an antique black telephone, with the other hand he tapped the receiver.

"OF ALL THE IMPERTINENT THINGS!" he hollered. "I apologize for my impatience, but our phones have been down all day! I'm told that it may be a couple days until the phone line is repaired. SO INCONVENIENT! It's because of all this blasted snow."

He slammed the phone down on the receiver and shoved it aside. Turning to his students, he smiled. "Here for orchestra rehearsal, eh? Anything I can do for you?"

Rollie, with the interjected help of his friends, told Yardsly about Zilch's secretary painting the wall and about how she had spotted them last night. He ended by telling about the hidden journal.

Yardsly's eyebrows rose high in surprise. "GOOD WORK! Where is the journal? Did you bring it with you?"

"We wanted to finish reading it for clues," said Rollie.

Yardsly smiled. "I appreciate your wanting to help, but it would be best to let the Yard experts study it as soon as possible. As for the secretary, there is no doubt she will report you to Zilch. This worries me." He rubbed his chin thoughtfully. "Your safety is my top priority. I will post Euston to guard your house, Rollie. Are the rest of you staying with the Wilsons right now?"

Wesley and Eliot nodded.

"I've been staying a few nights, but I live right down the street," Cecily informed him.

"STAY with the Wilsons," Yardsly advised. "Euston will watch over things. He'll investigate the vacant house, too—I'll give him a key to those pad-locks on the front door. Don't worry, you'll be safe with him. I may send someone to check on all of you in a few days, unless the phones get repaired. Then I'll just ring you."

With this new assurance, the sleuths relaxed and headed to the teachers' lounge for rehearsal. Miss Gram had slid aside the furniture to make room for chairs and music stands. A few other classmates sat in their assigned seats and tuned their instruments.

Mr. Chadwick A. Permiter greeted them at the door. "Happy New Year, kiddos!" The young American teacher bumped knuckles with each of them. "Or do you guys say 'Merry New Year'?"

"That sounds funny!" Cecily giggled. "Why would we say that?"

"Well, you British say *Happy* Christmas."

"You didn't go home to New York for the holi-days?" Rollie asked.

"Trying to get rid of me, huh?" Mr. Chad teased. "Nah, this year my family came here to visit me. They saved me a long trip home, and I gave them some English culture."

"Have they enjoyed their visit here?" asked Cecily.

Mr. Chad shrugged. "Yes and no. They've enjoyed hanging out with me and meeting Gwen, but they have not enjoyed driving on the wrong side of the road and having to convert dollars and cents to pounds and pence." He ushered them into the room. "Better get set up before Gwen starts growling."

"She growls?" Eliot asked in disbelief.

"Oh, yeah. Don't let that pretty little exterior fool you. Beneath that frilly disguise are claws."

"What are you saying about me, Chadwick?" Miss Gram cooed.

"Only that you're the sweetest creature ever." Mr. Chad smiled at her, then turned to the students and bared his teeth in warning.

Everyone stifled giggles. Miss Gram tapped her baton on her music stand.

Rollie, Cecily, Wesley, and Eliot made up the strings group in the orchestra—they all played the violin. A few years ago, Rollie and Cecily had signed up for lessons with a local violinist named Mrs. Trindle in the hopes of being more like Sherlock Holmes. They had quit lessons when they started at Sherlock Academy in August. They hadn't really minded quitting since neither cared much for the strict and overly perfumed Mrs. Trindle. But now they were a little excited to pick up their bows again and scratch out some music.

"Is everyone tuned?" Miss Gram checked over her small orchestra of fifteen students. "Let's run through the music." She indicated the sheet music on each stand and tapped her baton again. "Five, six, seven, eight!"

In response, a commotion of noise filled the small room. Miss Gram frowned, Mr. Chad winced, and the students nearly dropped their instruments.

"Do not lose heart," Miss Gram said. "Hence the reason for rehearsal. Let's try again, shall we?"

After a few tries, they successfully got through one piece of music. The second time through, however, when the last note ended, a saxophone could still be heard. Everyone turned to Arthur, one of the smallest boys at school, who did not let his speech impediment hold him back. The group watched in amusement as Arthur, lost in the music, swayed back and forth in his seat. His saxophone was almost as large as he was. He tapped his foot, closed his eyes, and proceeded to get carried away by a jazzy rendition of Blue Skies. Suddenly, he realized he was the only musician still playing. His eyes bugged open, and he turned a deep shade of red. Everyone clapped.

"That's *my* kind of music!" Mr. Chad voiced from a corner of the room. "American jazz!"

Miss Gram smiled at the small boy. "I had no idea you were so talented, Arthur. Perhaps you should have a solo."

Arthur shook his head. "No thank you, Miss Gwam."

"We'll see. Musicians, let's work out a few kinks in this piece." Miss Gram tapped her baton again for attention.

For the next hour, the orchestra practiced, and by the time Miss Gram released them for the day, they did not sound half bad. They carefully packed their instruments in their cases and bid Miss Gram good-bye.

Rollie and his friends were heading to the front door when Mr. Chad stopped them.

"Hold up there, kiddos." He beckoned them with his hand, a twinkle of mischief in his blue eyes. "Yardsly caught me up on what's been going on with you guys and MUS. First of all, I'm glad you're safe, Wes."

"Thank you, sir. I'm grateful for Rollie and his family taking me in."

"Amen to that. Cecily, how are you holding up with all these boys?"

Cecily giggled and blushed slightly. "I know how to hold my own."

"Tildster, have you been helping your friends?"

"I always help my friends, Mr. Chad. It's one of my rules I follow."

Mr. Chad grinned. "That's what I like to hear. And you, Rollie—are you glad for your comrades here?"

"Absolutely. We're really working as a team."

Mr. Chad nodded. "Listen, I know you guys are clever detectives, but even clever detectives need a little help, especially when they're not in school getting assistance from their teachers at the moment. So here's a little help." He flicked a business card between his fingers.

Rollie took the card and read it aloud: "Mycroft's Mercantile."

In a low mysterious voice, Mr. Chad elaborated, "It's a little hole-in-the-wall shop that specializes in detective and spy gear. They sell all kinds of supplies and gadgets. You never know when you'll need something extra to help with a case. Don't say I never gave you nothing."

"Where is this shop?" Rollie asked.

"Right around the corner on Siddons Lane. They've been closed for the holidays, but I think they're reopening tomorrow. By the way, the owner of the shop is an expert on all things detective—a real Sherlockian nut. He's a good guy. You can totally trust him. Good luck sleuths." He raised a high-five to them.

They all slapped his hand and bid him good-bye. They mounted the hansom cab waiting for them outside on the icy street.

"I really want to go to this shop," said Rollie. "Mycroft's Mercantile. I'll ask my dad if he can take us sometime this week." He slipped the business card into his coat pocket.

"Mycroft was Sherlock Holmes' only sibling. He was seven years older than Sherlock," Eliot clarified. "In case you didn't know."

Wesley grinned. "We know who Mycroft was. Any Sherlockian knows that."

"My fingertips are so sore from playing today," Cecily moaned. "I might get blisters!" She wrung her hand.

"You're a lefty?" Wesley grabbed her hand and scrutinized her small fingertips. "You need to rebuild your calluses."

"I do too, look." Eliot shoved his hand in Wesley's face, nearly poking him in the eye.

"Your fingers will have a week to rest until our next rehearsal," Rollie said. "When is Euston coming to my house?"

"Knowing Euston, he's probably already at your house," Wesley commented.

"Maybe we'll get a chance to ask him about the Holmes Brigade," Rollie said excitedly.

When they arrived at the Wilson manor, they felt a sense of security seeing Euston Hood posted on the front porch. His slim frame was clothed in his heavy, black coat, and an English cap topped his head. As they approached him, he nodded curtly and stepped aside to allow them to enter the house.

"Hello, Mr. Hood," Wesley greeted politely. "Thank you for watching over me again—I mean, all of us."

Euston's stony gaze softened, but he did not smile. "You're welcome, Mr. Livingston."

"We were wondering if you could tell us more about the Holmes Brigade."

Euston's brow furrowed. "What do you want to know?"

Rollie jumped in. "What does the Holmes Brigade do? Who else is in it?"

"It's a very secret society, so I cannot divulge too much. Every Holmes Brigade has had the same mission from its conception: to destroy MUS. The Brigade always consists of four members, no more and no less. The four members are selected Academy patrons."

The four children exploded with more questions:

"Besides you, who are the other three members?"

"How long have you been in the Brigade?"

"Can anyone join? Like us?"

"Do you have a secret handshake?"

Euston held up a gloved hand. "That's all I can tell you right now—but you may learn more very soon."

"Can we see your wristband?" asked Rollie.

Euston pulled up his sleeve to show them the leather band with the strange symbol. Then he waved them through the front door.

The four sleuths passed him and barged into the warm house. As they took off their coats and scarves, they chatted about their new bodyguard and his secret club.

"We're the perfect Brigade!" Rollie beamed. "There are already four of us."

Wesley nodded. "And we're current patrons—we're students."

"Our mission has always been to stop MUS," added Cecily.

"We need a secret handshake," Eliot decided. "I'll work on one."

"Euston won't stop us from exploring the house, will he?" Rollie wanted to know.

Wesley frowned. "He might. He takes his job of guarding very seriously. Maybe we can accompany him if he explores the house. Do we need to take another look?"

Rollie nodded. "It wouldn't hurt, especially since the secretary was back last night."

Eliot sighed. "I'm getting tired of that spooky house."

"You don't have to go with us," Cecily told him.

Eliot shook his head. "Oh, no, you can't leave me out like that."

"I'll talk with Euston and get a feel about us going next door." Wesley poked his head outside.

The other three headed to the dining room for lunch. Mr. and Mrs. Wilson had taken the girls into town to exchange some Christmas gifts. A stack of cold ham sandwiches wrapped in wax paper waited for them on the table. As they each grabbed one, Wesley came back.

"I don't think Euston will let us go. I got the feeling he means to keep us inside. We may need a diversion if we're gonna explore that house again."

All eyes turned to Eliot.

"What do you want *me* to do?"

"Go talk with him while we head out the back door," Rollie told him. "Keep him occupied for about ten minutes. We'll be quick."

"You didn't feel like going with us anyway," Cecily pointed out.

"But what am I going to talk to him about?" Eliot whined.

"Eliot, you can talk about anything to anyone for hours!" Rollie exclaimed with a chuckle. "Talk to him about all your rules."

"What rules?"

"Your rules for everything! Or see if you can get more out of him about the Holmes Brigade."

Wesley grinned. "We have every confidence in you."

Eliot sat up straight. "Very well, I'll do it for the team."

His friends patted him on the back and gobbled down their sandwiches.

Black and White Proof

"You know, Mr. Hood, we appreciate your watching over us, but it's not polite to be so quiet to your host. The rule is when you are staying at someone's house, you engage in a little conversation here and there. We're hoping you'll have more to say to us when you join the family for dinner tonight. I mean, you don't have to tell us your whole life story, but you could comment on the unusually snowy weather or compliment the meal. Did you ever take any etiquette classes? Well, I have. I'm taking Spy Etiquette and Interrogation at Sherlock Academy this year . . ."

Eliot yakked Euston's ear off as his comrades donned their winter clothing and crept out the back kitchen door.

Rollie led Wesley and Cecily across the snowy garden and out through the side gate. Seeing that

Euston's back was to them, they dodged next door and through Zilch's side gate. Crunching through the snow, they found the cellar window and dropped through it.

By now they knew the layout of the vacant house almost as well as the Wilson manor. They rushed upstairs and into the study at the end of the hallway. The drape was drawn closed, and the paint supplies still cluttered the center of the small room.

Rollie yanked off a mitten and ran his hand along the wall with the window. "She painted the whole wall except for around the window. That should be our top priority—figuring out why she's come back to paint the walls. I have an instinct that could be the key to this whole mystery of Zilch's missing list and whereabouts."

The three sleuths roamed the room, studying the walls, looking up at the ceiling. Wesley yanked open the drape again. Cecily knelt on the wooden-planked floor in hopes of finding footprints. Rollie inspected the paint supplies.

Squeak, creak!

Rollie stood in the center of the room and pressed his toes on the noisy floorboards. "This is the only section of the floor that squeaks." He knelt down to examine the wooden planks. "These floorboards are loose!"

Wesley and Cecily crowded around him. They worked their fingers into the seams and pried up a board. They gasped at the small cache beneath the floor. In the space, a small black attaché case was nestled. Rollie immediately reached down and brought the case up.

"It's not locked!" he said excitedly. He opened the lid.

The attaché case held several folders, papers, and photos. The three children sifted through the material.

"Wait, we need to be organized about this information," Wesley stopped them. "Let's look through one thing at a time carefully." He started with a folder.

"What about Eliot?" Cecily ran to the window and peered out. "He's looking impatient."

"Let's take this back to my house." Rollie closed the case and held it by its handle. "We can go through it in my room."

They hurriedly left Zilch's vacant house. Since soft snow was falling, they did not bother to cover their tracks. Once they were safely back at the Wilsons, Rollie raced to the front door.

Opening it, he announced, "Eliot, there you are! Stop bothering Mr. Hood."

Grateful, Eliot hurried inside. "It's about time! I was running out of things to say. He hardly said a word."

"You probably didn't let him." Cecily giggled. "Good work, Tildster!"

Eliot held up a warning finger at her. "The rule is only Mr. Chad can call me that. Did you guys find anything?"

Rollie held up the black attaché case, his brown eyes wide with excitement. "The game's afoot!" He galloped upstairs, his friends stampeding behind him.

Once in Rollie's little room, the detectives closed the door and assembled cross-legged on the carpet. Rollie put the case in the center of the circle. They all noted how new the case looked and reasoned that it must have been hidden under the floorboards more recently than the journal in the fireplace. Rollie opened the lid and pulled out the file folder on top.

The folder held a thick collection of newspaper clippings. Half of them heralded MUS accomplishments, the other half reported news on Sherlock Academy. They were thrilled to read articles about when the Academy first opened ten years ago, about the many fencing competitions its teams won, and about when the recess area was added on the roof five years ago.

Next, they opened a folder of old black-and-white photographs. Many were blurry portraits of people they did not recognize, and a majority of them had red X's scrawled over them. At the bottom, they came across a few people they did know.

"I think that's Euston!" Cecily observed. "It looks like him as a kid. He has that scar on his cheek."

"Why would Zilch have a photo of him?" asked Rollie.

"Euston said he had a previous connection to MUS," Wesley reminded him.

Cecily gasped very loudly. "Look at this photo!" She handed it to Rollie.

He gaped at the black-and-white photo that pictured a group of four people. He recognized all of them. Standing close together on the front steps of a large building were Herr Zilch, Headmaster Yardsly, his sister Ms. Yardsly, and none other than Auntie Ei. They all looked much younger than they did now.

Rollie gulped. "I don't believe it! Why are they in a photo together? I thought they all knew *of* Herr

Zilch, but this photo makes it look like they all knew him as a friend. And they're all smiling. I thought they were enemies."

"In his journal, Zilch mentioned that he used to be colleagues with Headmaster. Maybe he was colleagues with Ms. Yardsly and Auntie Ei, too." Cecily studied the photo closer. "I can barely see the sign on the building behind them, but I think it says Scotland Yard."

"Did they all work for Scotland Yard long ago?" Wesley wondered.

"Auntie Ei still works a little with them," Rollie answered. "I don't know about the others."

"Headmaster has police training," Eliot said matter-of-factly. "Rupert told me."

"I have a hard time believing Zilch worked for Scotland Yard," Rollie muttered. "He's a bad guy."

"Maybe he wasn't always on the wrong side of the law," Cecily said.

"He's quite a mystery, isn't he?" said Wesley.

"So is Auntie Ei." Rollie frowned. His growing distrust of Auntie Ei intensified after seeing this photo of her with Zilch. There was a past history there, shrouded in secrets. Auntie Ei was guarding those secrets, and he did not know why.

A horrible thought wormed its way into his mind. He tried to ward it off, but it wiggled through. Perhaps Auntie Ei was a double agent—perhaps she was working with MUS! The photo showed Zilch and Auntie Ei together. Zilch did not want Rollie to attend Sherlock Academy, and it seemed neither did Auntie Ei. Had she only consented to use Rollie as an MUS spy without him knowing it—just like Wesley?

"You should ask your aunt about this photo," said Wesley.

Rollie shook his head. "She won't tell me anything, and she'll get mad at us for going next door. She told me it was useless." He suddenly brightened. "I'll bet Uncle Ky knows something about this photo. We can ask him."

Cecily sneezed three times in a row. She wiped her nose on her pocket handkerchief. "I think I caught a little chill in that house. It's so cold and dusty."

Rollie eyed her for a moment, then whipped out his pocket notepad and pencil stub. "So here are the facts we know:

- **Herr Zilch has a past with the Yardslys and Auntie Ei . . . maybe at Scotland Yard**
- **His secretary has returned to paint the study**

• **The MUS list is still at large**

Did I leave out anything?"

"Yes." Wesley nodded. "Herr Zilch knows we know about his secretary."

Rollie grimaced and added this fact to his list. "We've got to be extra alert and careful now. Even with Euston here, we may not be entirely safe from Zilch."

Another Prowler
in the House

Dinner that night was a little awkward because the ever silent Euston Hood joined the family at the table. Mrs. Wilson thought the whole situation with him guarding their house was very irregular. She watched him chew the lamb stew, hoping for the smallest sign that he liked the dinner. He did not reveal any emotions. Lucille and Daphne stared at him through the whole meal until Uncle Ky elbowed them to stop. Edward and Stewart did not seem to even notice Euston; they gobbled down their stew without taking a breath. Auntie Ei did not give Euston any attention; she darted her eyes at Rollie a few times. He met her gaze once but decided he would not do that again—it made him feel guiltier.

"Mr. Hood, we're honored to have you with us," Mr. Wilson ventured after clearing his throat. "Is this your regular line of work—being a bodyguard?"

Euston nodded and swallowed another bite.

"Is it a fact you work with Headmaster Yardsly?"

Another nod.

"How long have you worked with him?"

Euston wiped his mouth on his napkin. "For many years."

Eliot rolled his eyes. "Remember what we talked about this afternoon? About engaging in polite conversation?"

Euston flashed him an annoyed look, the first expression he had made so far. He polished off his bowlful, wiped his mouth, and stood. "Thank you for the meal. It was excellent." With that, he bundled up and resumed his post outside in the dark snowy night.

"That Mr. Hood is most peculiar!" Mrs. Wilson exclaimed. "I offered him a cot in the library by the fireplace, and he refused. He's going to sleep on the floor in the entry hall right in front of the front door. I feel obligated to show him hospitality in exchange for his services, but he won't accept it."

"Fact: You need not get worked up over it, Eloise." Mr. Wilson glanced up at her from his bowl. "Let the man be. Some people are just quiet souls."

"I have no idea what that means," Edward said as he chewed on bread and butter.

"Fact: I'm afraid you never will, son," Mr. Wilson quipped.

Rollie spoke up. "Dad, there's this shop near school that we really want to go to. It sells detective stuff. Could you take us sometime this week?"

"It is called Mycroft's Mercantile," Auntie Ei abruptly croaked.

Rollie snapped his eyes at her in surprise before he could stop himself. "You know about that shop? You never told me."

"Another secret I have been hoarding," the old lady retorted sharply.

"Let's go tomorrow, son," Mr. Wilson decided.

Cecily sneezed into her napkin.

"Bless you!" a chorus of voices responded.

"Cecily, let me feel your forehead." Mrs. Wilson reached over and placed the back of her hand against Cecily's pale forehead. "You feel a little warm, and your cheeks are flushed."

"I don't feel good," Cecily admitted meekly.

"I think you had better go right to bed." Mrs. Wilson stood and beckoned Cecily to follow her. "I don't want you getting terribly ill."

Without a word, Cecily followed Mrs. Wilson out the dining room and upstairs.

"Is she sick?" Eliot screeched in panic. "I do NOT want to get sick! I probably will! I've been in close proximity with her for days now. We need to sterilize your room, Rollie."

Everyone except for Auntie Ei laughed.

"This is no laughing matter!" Eliot looked shocked at them. He bolted up and fled the dining room.

"I'm sure Cecily will be fine," Mr. Wilson assured them. "She probably just caught a chill from outside. You've been playing out in the snow a lot lately. Building more snow forts?"

Rollie and Wesley exchanged glances.

Rollie shrugged. "And other things."

Auntie Ei shot them a sharp look.

As the family dispersed, Rollie followed Uncle Ky into the parlor. The elderly man sat down to work on the jigsaw puzzle.

"Uncle Ky, could you help me with something?"

"Ah, you're on a case, aren't you? Well, I was never a professional detective, but I have done my fair share of investigating in my day. I once tailed an Oxford student who I suspected was changing the time on a clock as a prank. Turned out that particular time piece was broken. High-maintenance contraptions, clocks are. What can I help you with, Rollin Holmes?"

Rollie fished out the black-and-white photograph from his pocket and showed it to his great-uncle. "Did Auntie Ei work for Scotland Yard a long time ago?"

Uncle Ky's face clouded. "Where did you find this photograph? I have not seen it in years. I think Eileen keeps it hidden."

"It's not hers—at least, I don't think it is. I know she still works with Scotland Yard a little, but did she used to work with them full-time? Along with everyone else in this photo?"

"Before Sherlock Academy opened, Eileen and the others shown here worked for Scotland Yard—inspectors they were. Almost all the Academy staff once worked for Scotland Yard at some time. Then when the Academy opened, they chose to retire from the Yard and teach, you know."

Rollie got excited. "Even this man? He used to be a Yard inspector?" He pointed to Herr Zilch.

"Yes, they had all been a part of a highly secret division of Scotland Yard—a sort of secret society. I believe that man in question had a falling out with everyone. I daresay he was fired from the Yard—Eileen had something to do with that. I am not entirely sure what happened to him. It was a very long time ago, as you can tell by how much younger everyone looks." Uncle Ky shifted his attention back to the puzzle.

Rollie slipped the photograph back in his pocket and headed upstairs. The history involving his great-aunt and his archenemy was beginning to take form. The two of them, including the Yardsly siblings, had worked together, had been comrades. They had gone on to work at Sherlock Academy—except for Herr Zilch. Something had happened, a disagreement or a fight. Herr Zilch had been fired and henceforth hated the Academy. Maybe that was how Zilch had gotten involved with MUS. Auntie Ei had had something to do with it all.

Rollie fished out the photograph again to study it. He noticed a minute detail he had overlooked before. He could barely make it out . . .

He ran upstairs and flew into his room.

Eliot was wiping down everything imaginable. The air smelled of bleach.

"That's strong!" Wesley was nearly gagging.

"It has to be strong to kill the germs," Eliot panted, feverishly scrubbing the desk. "You'll thank me later when you stay healthy while Cecily is sick in bed."

Rollie rummaged around in his desk drawer until he found his magnifying glass. He studied the photograph through it. "Take a look at this!"

Wesley and Eliot peered through the magnifying glass, and gasped.

"They're all wearing wristbands!" Wesley exclaimed. "I can't see any symbols on them—"

"Uncle Ky just told me that the four of them were part of a secret division of Scotland Yard. They were part of the Holmes Brigade!"

Eliot shook his head. "Euston said the Brigades were made up of current Academy patrons. Herr Zilch was never a patron."

"Or was he?" asked Wesley. "We never thought Zilch was a Yard inspector, or even more, part of the Holmes Brigade."

"So the Brigade is a secret division of Scotland Yard," Rollie deduced. "This is becoming more and more interesting!"

"And confusing," Eliot mumbled.

"I hope Cecily is better tomorrow," Rollie said. "I can't wait to tell her about this."

But the next morning, Cecily was not better; she was worse. She was running a high fever, her throat hurt when she swallowed, and her nose was stuffy. Mrs. Wilson moved Lucille and Daphne downstairs to the parlor to give Cecily rest. The little girls did not mind, for they enjoyed camping out downstairs. Daphne cheerfully gave up her bed to Cecily. Being the mother of five children, who had had their share of illnesses, Mrs. Wilson was the perfect nurse. She kept Cecily comfortable and hydrated, letting her rest but also checking on her every few hours. She forbade the boys from bothering her. The boys thought it only fair to postpone their trip to Mycroft's Mercantile until Cecily was well enough to join them.

"She's gonna be okay, right Mum?" Rollie asked, a little worried.

"She just has a cold. She'll be feeling better by tomorrow, I'm sure. Keep your voices down so she can sleep."

While Rollie enjoyed the company of Wesley and Eliot, he missed her. He and Cecily had been friends for so long and had worked on so many cases together that he had come to rely on her input. She tended to point out details he missed, to voice concerns he failed to consider, and to rally him on when he needed extra courage. He hoped she would not be sick too much longer.

Rollie rejoined his friends in his bedroom. They sprawled on the floor, working on their Independent Study homework. "Cecily's got a cold."

"I told you!" Eliot preached. "Now aren't you glad I bleached your room?"

"I need a break." Wesley yawned. "We've been working all morning. Want to get some fresh air?"

Rollie smiled. "By fresh air, do you mean explore the vacant house again?"

Wesley grinned back. "We've already found two hiding spaces with Zilch's secrets. There could be more."

"I don't want to distract Euston again," Eliot whined. "It was so exhausting!"

"Let's see where he is," Rollie said. "We might be able to sneak past him."

The three boys tiptoed down the hall, past Cecily's sick room, and downstairs. Rollie peeked out the narrow window beside the front door.

"I don't see him. Maybe he's in the back."

They hurried into their coats, scarves, boots, and mittens. Outside, a soft snow fell. Rollie led the way down the front walkway to the street. Still seeing no sign of Euston, they scampered next door, through the garden gate, and into the back garden. They entered the house the usual way through the cellar window.

Since they had not explored downstairs much, they started in the grand formal entry hall. They headed into a large room off the right, which they concluded must have been a parlor. White sheets shrouded a settee and two armchairs with gold and scarlet upholstery. Wesley and Eliot pressed their toes along the marble tile. Rollie poked around the grand fireplace large enough for him to stand in. They were disappointed to find no secret hiding places of any kind. Rollie headed for the doorway but suddenly stopped, causing his friends to bump into him.

"Someone's coming down the stairs," he whispered.

Cautiously, they each peeked through the doorway.

Euston silently padded down the stairs and toward the front double-doors. He gripped a manila file folder in one hand. He let himself out through the front doors, clicking the locks closed behind him. When he was gone, the boys quietly tiptoed out of the parlor.

"What was he doing upstairs?" whispered Rollie.

"He was probably just checking everything out," Wesley whispered back. "Yardsly wanted him to. He said he'd give Euston a key, remember?"

"He had a folder though. Does it belong to him or did he find it upstairs?" Rollie entered another large room across the entry hall, which boasted empty bookshelves. "Let's finish investigating the first floor. Libraries are great places for secret hiding spots."

The boys searched the spacious built-in bookshelves, the ornate mantel and fireplace, the carpeted floor—nothing turned up. They finished searching the dining room that boasted a coat of arms above its fireplace, the coat closet that housed only a dusty broom, and the kitchen with its black stove and bare cupboards. Finding nothing, they climbed back through the cellar window.

"I guess there are no more secret hiding spots," Rollie muttered. "I think Euston found that folder upstairs, which means it belongs to Herr Zilch. And if it belongs to him, then it must contain more secrets. We need every extra secret we can get. Hopefully there will be a clue about the MUS list."

"I agree." Wesley closed the garden gate behind them. "We need to get that folder from Euston."

"Shh! There he is." Rollie crouched down behind the low brick wall that separated Zilch's front yard from his.

The boys spotted Euston standing rigid on the front porch. He was flipping through the papers in the folder.

"How do we get back to your place?" Eliot whispered. "He'll see us coming and will know we were in the house."

Rollie bent low and crept through the snow back to Zilch's garden gate. Once through the gate, he stood up and said, "We'll have to climb over into my back garden. Then we can go through the kitchen door."

Eliot spotted some empty wooden crates under the leafless willow tree near the back wall. The boys stacked the three crates. Without hesitation, Wesley climbed to the top of the stack. At the top, he easily scrambled onto the brick wall, looked left and right, and then dropped down over the side. Rollie and Eliot heard a crunch of snow and a grunt. Next, Rollie climbed up and over. He had barely hit the snow on the other side when Eliot landed beside him. They hurried through the back door and into the kitchen.

As they wiggled out of their winter garb, Wesley asked, "So how are we going to get that folder from Euston?"

Rollie licked his lips. "I'm not sure yet, but I know we can come up with a plan."

The Mystery in the Folder

They did come up with a plan.

By now, Euston had made himself quite at home on the Wilson's front porch. A low stool and wooden crate served as his chair and desk. A tin canteen of water, a paper bag of peanuts, and a flashlight cluttered the top of the crate. Atop this crate also rested the file folder from Zilch's house.

If Euston would not leave the porch, Rollie would have to make him leave. He went to his mother's workroom where she was sewing.

"Mum, you should invite Mr. Hood in for some afternoon tea," said Rollie. "It's really cold outside, and I think it's about to snow again."

Mrs. Wilson frowned and looked up from her sewing machine. "Rollie, I've tried. He said he would only impose on us for dinner. *Impose* was his word!

He is not imposing at all. I want to be hospitable, but he doesn't seem to want it."

"Maybe he wouldn't mind just coming in to warm himself by the fire for a few minutes. Should I invite him in?"

Mrs. Wilson aligned the fabric under the needle. "Be my guest. Oh! Tell Mr. Hood that."

Rollie rejoined his friends in the entry hall. "Mum already invited him in, but he declined."

"Our plan won't work unless he leaves the porch," Wesley reminded them. "Or we do plan B." He turned to Eliot.

Eliot rolled his eyes. "Fine, but I won't like it one bit—and neither will Euston." With a grunt, he dressed warmly and went outside.

"What do you want now, Mr. Tildon?" Euston muttered in his deep voice.

"Well, I . . . uh . . . " Eliot stammered for perhaps the first time in his life. "I would like some advice on how to be a better sleuth. You seem very knowledgeable and stealthy and I would like to learn how to be more like you. Being more stealthy could really aid me as a detective . . . "

"Is he turning away from the crate?" whispered Wesley.

Rollie nodded. Ever so slowly, he eased open the front door. Squatting, he edged out onto the porch and toward the crate, all the while keeping an eye on Euston's back. Eliot played his part well, never once glancing at Rollie behind Euston. He chatted on and on, using animated gestures and direct eye contact to keep Euston facing him.

Rollie was almost to the crate.

Rollie's fingers touched the file folder and snatched it up. He whipped around to check on Euston. The quiet man was nodding at Eliot. Rollie edged back inside the house and handed the folder to Wesley.

Wesley flipped open the folder and found two sheets of paper inside. One paper had typed text and the other had a blueprint. Wesley was ready with his own pocket notepad and pencil. At a remarkable speed, he copied down the text from the folder paper to his notepad. Since there were only a few lines, it only took him a few moments. Next, he placed another paper atop the blueprint and started to trace it.

"Wait a minute." He paused. "This is a blueprint of Sherlock Academy!"

Rollie studied it. "You're right! Don't copy it. I have a blueprint of school on my old newspaper map. Let's get this folder back to Euston's crate."

Wesley stuffed the papers back in the folder and handed it to his friend.

Rollie poked his head out the front door.

"Mr. Tildon, if you will just let me speak I will—"

"One last thing, Mr. Hood. I've been wondering lately if I need to have a deep dark secret to make myself more interesting and mysterious. Holmes had lots of great secrets, and I just think that maybe I need one. That seems to be the rule. *You're* part of the secret Holmes Brigade. But I can't think of any secrets. I don't belong to any secret societies and I don't have any treasures to hide—I'm not wealthy. Well, I do get birthday money from my father, but that's really not much to speak of. I don't have any eccentric relatives that are spies or anything . . . "

Rollie edged back across the porch.

Creak!

The front door squeaked on its hinges.

Euston started to turn his head.

"Mr. Hood! I almost forgot! I do have a secret! Let me tell you it and you can decide if it's worth using to define myself as a detective. Please?"

Euston sighed. "Go ahead."

Rollie slid the file folder back onto the crate and crawled back inside. He wiped his glistening forehead, and then he signaled Eliot to rejoin them inside.

"On second thought, Mr. Hood, I don't think I should tell you my secret because then it wouldn't be a secret anymore. That's how secrets work, you know. Nice talking with you." With a wave, Eliot darted into the house. "I hope you were successful because I am NOT doing that again."

"We were. Let's go to my room." Rollie led his friends upstairs. On his way down the hall, he paused at Cecily's door. It was open a crack, so he peeked in.

Since the room was dark, he could not tell if she was awake or not. He guessed she was sleeping, since she did not acknowledge him and she was breathing deeply. He continued down the hall and up the twelve steps to his room.

"So what was in the folder?" asked Eliot.

Wesley laid his notepad on the desk.

"What's this supposed to be?" Eliot pointed to the paper with the half-traced blueprint.

"That's a blueprint of Sherlock Academy," explained Wesley. "But I didn't finish tracing it because Rollie said he already had a blueprint of school."

Rollie rummaged around under his bed for his large hollow Shakespeare book. He opened it and dug around inside. Frowning, he shoved aside Auntie Ei's letters to Yardsly that he had taken from school. He pulled out an antique newspaper. He separated the yellow pages and spent the next few minutes shuffling them around on his bed.

Wesley and Eliot flanked him and gazed upon a black ink sketch of the Academy's floor plans. The page corners were matched like a puzzle to complete the sketch.

"Brilliant!" Wesley grinned. "Did your aunt give you this?"

Rollie nodded. "It's how I found the secret passage at school."

"Let me see this closer." Eliot leaned down, his nose almost touching the pages.

"Later, Eliot." Rollie gathered the pages into a neat stack again. "Let's read this other page from the folder."

"It doesn't make any sense." Wesley folded his arms.

Orwjc Yaxkunv rw yaxppanbb. NCJ: oren vxwcqb.

"Crikey, it's in code!" Eliot laughed. "Finally! A code I can work on."

"You think you can crack it?" Rollie raised his eyebrows.

"Codes are my specialty. It will take some time though. I'll need to make a decoder ring. It looks like Zilch assigned letters to represent different letters."

Wesley and Rollie stared blankly at him.

"For example, this word—if that's what you can call it—*oren* must represent other letters. If we can figure out which letter Zilch assigned to be a, b, c, and so forth, then we can substitute his letters for the real alphabet and crack the code."

Rollie patted Eliot's back. "We'll leave that to you, since codes are your specialty."

"Thank you! I'll get to work right away. Don't bother me!" Eliot grabbed the coded message, his notepad, and his pencil, and he headed off to the library downstairs.

"Why did Zilch have a blueprint of the Academy?" asked Wesley.

"I'm sure we'll know more when Eliot decodes that message. Maybe he was hoping to find the secret passage. That's what he had you looking for, remember?"

Wesley nodded solemnly.

"You need to let that go." Rollie cocked his head to one side. "How Zilch used you—let it go. It's in the past."

"I have a hard time letting the past go."

Rollie thought for a moment. "You know who else has a hard time letting the past go? Herr Zilch. He must still be bitter at his nephew for betraying him. Perhaps that's why he hates the Academy so much. He also has not let the past history of Holmes defeating Moriarty go. He still lives in fear of that. He's let the past define who he is."

"You're right. Thanks, mate, for everything. For forgiving me, for letting me stay here, for being a great friend. I needed a good friend like you."

"What are you talking about? You're the most popular boy at school! You have lots of friends, don't you?"

Wesley shrugged. "I know a lot of people, and a lot of people know me. But being popular doesn't mean you have real friends. You've turned out to be a true friend."

The boys worked on Independent Study homework until dinner. At dinner Rollie felt a little nervous sitting close to Euston; he wondered if Euston suspected what they had done. Eliot refused to join the family for dinner. He insisted on working to crack the code, pausing briefly to snack on a piece of bread and cold chicken. Mrs. Wilson fed Cecily soup upstairs.

After dinner, Rollie was waiting in the hall when his mother came out of the girls' bedroom, an empty soup bowl in hand.

"She's much better," Mrs. Wilson assured him. "She wants to talk to you, but keep it brief. She needs to go back to sleep."

Rollie slipped into the dim bedroom. The ballerina lamp on the white bedside table between his sisters' canopy beds cast a cozy glow. Cecily lay in Daphne's bed, her head propped up on a pillow and her body snug beneath the lavender bedspread.

"How are you feeling?" Rollie asked politely.

"Ugh! Being sick isn't fud!" Cecily sniffed.

"You mean *fun*?" teased Rollie. "You're nose is really stuffed up!"

Cecily glared at him. "I read by notes frob last subber on Zilch—when he was Crenshaw. I foud a code I copied frob hib."

"A code? Eliot's cracking a coded message from Zilch right now!" Rollie excitedly told her what they had been up to. "Maybe that code in your notes could help him."

"I hope so!" Cecily held out her open notebook to him. "Give this to Eliot. I hope to be better id the bording."

"In the morning?" Rollie clarified with a grin.

Cecily blew her nose on a tissue. "Don't bake fud of be!"

Rollie closed the bedroom door behind him and skipped downstairs to the library. There he found Eliot sprawled on his stomach on the carpet, papers and his open code textbook surrounding him.

"Cecily found some old codes she had copied down from Zilch last summer," Rollie said as he dropped the open notebook in front of his friend. "Maybe these can help."

"Crikey! This looks like the same code. This is helpful." Eliot scratched his head of shaggy raven hair. "Go on to bed. I'm going to work well into the night if I have to."

"Good luck, chum."

Rollie took the first shift to watch for Zilch's secretary to return next door. He sat at his desk and wondered if she dared to now that they had seen her and now that Euston was guarding the area.

He thought about Herr Zilch. While he had learned a great deal about the criminal over the past week, he still did not understand Zilch's past. What did Auntie Ei have to do with Herr Zilch being fired from Scotland Yard? Did this have something to do with the reason Zilch hated the Academy and had become leader of Moriarty's Underground Society?

Why did Zilch have a photograph of Euston? Was he targeting the bodyguard? Euston was Yardsly's agent, so he was obviously a threat to MUS. Maybe Zilch was hunting the quiet man down. Maybe it had something to do with Euston being a part of this mysterious Holmes Brigade. Euston seemed capable of taking care of himself, so Rollie did not worry too much for his safety.

But he did worry for the safety of his family, his friends, and himself. Zilch had once threatened to harm Rollie's loved ones if he did not stay out of Zilch's way. Zilch had already attacked Wesley. Now he knew that Rollie and his friends knew about the secretary. Rollie shuddered.

And what about that secretary? Why had she returned to paint the study walls? It was inexplicable! Since it was the only room that she was painting, Rollie knew there had to be a good reason for it. Was there a secret in the walls?

Rollie gasped.

"Is she back?" Wesley's hoarse voice sounded from the floor.

"No, I just thought of something."

Rollie was about to share his revelation with Wesley when suddenly the light next door blared on. Instinctively, he ducked below his desk.

Wesley eased up to peek through the window. "It's her! She's not painting. She just taped an envelope on the windowpane. She's looking up at your window. I think it's for us! She's gone."

The light turned off, and Rollie popped up. Through the pale moonlight, he could faintly see a white square against the window in Zilch's study.

As Rollie scooted into bed, he said, "It's from Herr Zilch, I'm sure."

"I'm dying to read it!" Wesley whispered. "Should we go get it?"

Rollie shook his head. "It's way too risky. Euston's sleeping in the entry hall, so we can't get our coats, and the secretary could still be prowling around."

"You're right. We'll get it first thing in the morning."

"What does Herr Zilch want?"

A Threat, a Puzzle,
and a Solution

"E liot? Eliot!"
Rollie knelt on the library floor and shook the sleeping boy.

Eliot jolted and sat upright. His shaggy hair stuck up, and the carpet texture was imprinted on his cheek. He rubbed his tired eyes, and glanced around at the pool of papers drowning him.

"It's morning," said Rollie.

Eliot yawned. "I'm close to cracking the code."

After catching Eliot up on the secretary's return, Rollie and Wesley decided to retrieve the letter before Euston found it. They scrambled into their winter outerwear while Eliot stumbled to the dining room for some breakfast. They were a little alarmed when they couldn't find Euston. Hoping he was not next door, the two sleuths raced through the snow to the cellar window.

Encountering no one, they arrived in the study upstairs to find the envelope still taped on the windowpane. Wesley snatched it and turned to leave, but Rollie lingered to stare at one of the unpainted walls.

"What's the matter, Rollie?"

"I thought of something last night. These walls must have some sort of secret if the secretary is going to all that trouble to paint over them. That secret could be the MUS list!"

Wesley stared at the wall with Rollie. "I can't see anything."

"Maybe the list is hidden *in* the walls, and the secretary is painting over them to cover up some clue about how to open the paneling."

"That sounds like Zilch. He likes hiding things in secret places. We need some tools if we're going to pry open this paneling."

Rollie ran his hand along the wall, hoping for something to give way. He reached the end and continued along the second unpainted wall. No panels were loose, nothing budged. He noted that funny smell again though.

"Should we get to work on these walls?" asked Wesley.

"I don't know. The other hiding places—the one in the fireplace and the one under the floorboards—were easy to open and pretty accessible. I would think if there was a secret hiding place behind the paneling, it would be the same way. There must be something else we're not thinking of."

"Zilch's journal was hidden in the bedroom fireplace—maybe this fireplace has a secret." Wesley poked around the small fireplace. "Nothing here." He stuffed the envelope into his coat pocket and led Rollie back through the drafty old house.

As they tramped down the hall, they collided into Euston.

"Hello, Mr. Hood," Wesley greeted, his voice a little high with surprise.

"Mr. Livingston, Mr. Wilson." Euston studied them. "It is my duty to protect you. I cannot do that when I don't know where you are. You must stay home. I do not want to find you here again. You're trespassing, and it's dangerous. Do I make myself clear?"

The boys gulped and nodded.

"How did you know we were here?" asked Rollie.

"Your tracks in the snow. I suspected you were sneaking over here but could not catch you at it. Then I saw your trail this morning. I'll escort you home." Placing a gloved hand on each boy's shoulder, Euston accompanied them out through the front doors. He did not bother removing his grip on them to lock up the doors behind them. He did not say another word as he escorted them back to the Wilson manor and watched them enter the house.

"That's great!" Rollie groaned. "Just when we're onto an important clue with those study walls, we get grounded. Well, we're not going to let him get in the way of solving this case—it's too important for the sake of our school!"

They found Eliot back in the library, looking much refreshed and working hard on the code.

"I've almost got it!"

Rollie and Wesley joined him on the floor. Wesley tore open the envelope.

"I see you've been busy detectives!" a new voice sounded at the door.

Cecily entered the library. She was dressed in a green cardigan and her brother's old trousers, the hems cuffed. Her usually healthy glow had returned to her freckled cheeks. Besides her voice sounding a bit nasally, she appeared to be back in good health.

Rollie smiled. "Cecily! We have a message from Zilch. Open it, Wesley."

Wesley slipped out a single sheet of paper from the envelope. He read it aloud:

Sleuths,

It seems I underestimated you. My secretary has important business to attend to in my old residence. It would be wise of you to stay out of her way. Consider this a warning to leave my property alone. If you fail to heed my warning, I will have no choice but to accompany her and thus ensure you do not get in our way again. You will not thwart me this time!

—Herr Zilch

"Now I'm nervous," Wesley admitted.

"I've cracked the code!" Eliot whooped triumphantly.

"Were my notes helpful?" asked Cecily.

Eliot nodded emphatically. "Absolutely helpful! Once I figured out Zilch had started his alphabet with *j* for *a*, and *k* for *b*, and *l* for *c*, and—"

"We get it, Eliot! What's it say?" Rollie asked breathlessly.

"It's still somewhat of a riddle. It says, 'Final Problem in progress. ETA: five months.'" Eliot blinked at them.

Wesley asked the obvious. "What's the Final Problem?"

"Whatever it is, it's going to happen in five months," Rollie muttered. "Five months from when?"

"It sounds ominous for sure," Cecily noted. "A little doomsday-ish."

"The Final Problem is the title of the case in which Holmes and Moriarty fought," said Rollie. "Moriarty was defeated . . . "

"Maybe this Final Problem is some elaborate plan to ultimately defeat Sherlock Academy," Cecily suggested. "That's always been Zilch's end goal, right?"

"And this message was attached to that blueprint of school," said Wesley.

"We *have* to find that MUS list." Rollie rubbed his eyes.

"There are no new clues about where it might be?" Cecily asked.

Wesley sighed. "We thought the message could be hidden behind the study walls. We haven't removed the paneling yet because we thought there should be an opening or something."

"And there's nothing written on the walls?" Cecily narrowed her eyes.

"No, nothing, but there has to be some reason the secretary is painting the walls."

Everyone sat quietly, feeling a little disheartened by Zilch's threat, by the mystery at hand, and by the dead end they seemed to be at.

Rollie tried to ignore the presence of his friends and engage his brain in some good, hard thinking. He was not used to working on a case with so many others; he was having a hard time focusing his brain long enough to make any deductions. He remembered Holmes always needed solitude to think through the clues. Holmes once joked he wanted to lock himself in a box to be alone with his thoughts. That appealed to Rollie right then. Since it would take too long to scrounge up a box big enough for him and it would most likely alarm his friends, he closed his eyes and clapped his hands over his ears.

Rollie knew he was overlooking something, some detail. Holmes always said to pay attention to the tiniest details, for therein could lie the answer to any mystery.

So what were the details? The walls held a secret. The secretary was painting over them to hide the secret. The secret could be the MUS list. Rollie discarded his original idea that the list was hidden behind the walls. If it were, the secretary could just open the paneling and remove the list.

No, the list had to be irremovable. It had to be preserved in such a way that only painting over the walls could hide it—assuming the list was the secret she was covering. Well, no matter the secret, if it was worth covering up, it was worth finding.

There was no writing on the walls, no drawings, no symbols, nothing. Just plain paneled walls.

It was as if the secret was invisible . . . unless one knew where to look.

Rollie snapped to attention. An idea shot through his brain. It was just a guess, but it was the best he had come up with so far.

"I've got it!" he shouted, causing his friends to jump. "I know where the list is!"

"Zilch just threatened us to abandon this case," Cecily said quietly. "I think we had better do just that."

Rollie shook his head. "We need to check something first! We're very close; I can sense it. We need to try one last thing on those walls."

"Euston just grounded us," Wesley reminded him. "There's too much at risk here."

Rollie stood up. "There's always risk when you're a detective. The safety of Sherlock Academy is always worth the risk." He took off running upstairs.

His friends chased after him. In his room, he dove under the bed and slid out his hollow Shakespeare book. He opened the cover and rummaged around inside.

"What are you looking for?" Eliot demanded.

"The solution to invisible ink!"

Mycroft's Mercantile

"The MUS list is invisible!" Rollie explained.

Rollie's friends gaped at him.

"You mean the list is written in invisible ink on the walls?" asked Wesley.

"Like my PS?" questioned Eliot.

"Exactly!" Rollie held up his pipe. "And we have the solution."

"That makes sense!" Cecily agreed excitedly. "That's why the secretary has to paint over the list instead of taking it with her. And she has to paint over all the walls because she's not quite sure where the list is written—"

Rollie grinned. "Because it's totally invisible!"

"How are we going to reveal the list?" Eliot asked doubtfully. "Those walls are spacious. We can't just sprinkle the solution all over them. This won't work."

"A minor detail." Rollie glanced out his window at the vacant house. "We can figure this out."

"I know how we can do it." Wesley brightened. "We can use a paintbrush like the secretary does. We'll dip the paintbrush in the solution and wipe the walls down with it."

"Brilliant!" Cecily praised.

"Elementary!" Rollie smiled back.

"There's not enough solution for that." Eliot shook his head. "The pipe holds only about three tablespoons. We need to get more somehow. Does anyone know how to make the solution?"

Cecily turned to Wesley. "Have you taken a chemistry class?"

"Not yet. I signed up to take Sherlockian Chemistry this next semester."

"I know where we can get more though," Rollie said, his brown eyes widening with excitement. "Mycroft's Mercantile! Let's ask my dad to take us."

They found Mr. Wilson with Uncle Ky in the parlor. The two men sat hunched over the card table and snapped puzzle pieces into place. The landscape puzzle of the Lake District was nearly complete.

"Dad! Can you take us to that detective shop? Please? We really need to buy something. It's important to our case."

"Hmm?"

"Dad! Please?"

Mr. Wilson dragged his eyes away from the puzzle to look at his son. "Right now? Why not tomorrow?"

"No, Dad, we need to go now! We really need something."

"Fact: Sleuth work comes first." Mr. Wilson sighed and looked helplessly at Uncle Ky. "Very well, get your coats." He stood and ushered them to the front door. "Eloise! I'm taking the children into town for a bit!" he hollered as he opened the front door. "Did you hear that fact, lovey?"

"I heard you, Peter!" Mrs. Wilson's voice rang from the back of the sprawling house. "Be a love and pick me up some sewing needles!"

"Let's go, sleuths." Mr. Wilson ushered everyone outside. "Mr. Hood, I'm taking the children into town for an hour or two. Is that alright with you?"

"Yes, sir. Safe travels." Euston tipped his cap.

Mr. Wilson led the group to the right side of the house where the family's navy automobile was parked. He and the boys cleared off fresh snow from the windshield. Rollie joined his father in the front while his three friends piled into the back seat. With a sleepy putter, the car headed toward the city.

"Where is this shop, son?"

Rollie bit his lip. "It's right around the corner from school. I'm not sure where exactly."

"Where's that business card Mr. Chad gave you?" Cecily asked from the back seat.

Rollie dug around in his coat pockets. He pulled out a wad of tissue, paper scraps, a rubber band, and a stray button.

Mr. Wilson chuckled. "Fact: You are definitely my son. Mum cleans out my coat pockets every evening when I get home from the college."

Rollie smiled sheepishly as he found the business card. "Here it is. The address is 34 Siddons Lane. Do you know that street, Dad?"

"Fact: It's a little side lane near Baker Street. What's so important that you need to have right now?"

"We need a solution to invisible ink," answered Rollie.

The rest of the ride into town the group chit-chatted about rugby and Uncle Ky and Euston Hood. Everyone was surprised to learn from Wesley that Euston was only twenty-five. They all agreed that while he looked young, he acted much older.

They passed an icy Regent's Park and a nearly frozen boat lake. Soon they drove down Baker Street, bypassing Sherlock Academy. They took an immediate right onto Siddons Lane and headed down the correct side to find number 34. The lane was very tight, crammed with an assortment of small businesses. They almost passed Mycroft's Mercantile, for it was a small shop sandwiched between an Irish pub and a Chinese dry cleaner. A small display window boasted a sign with the shop's name. Mr. Wilson thought it very lucky to find a parking spot right in front of the shop. After killing the engine, he led his posse to the shop's green door. The door hit a little bell as it opened.

The shop was very narrow, more like a closet than a proper store. Shelves crammed with everything from toothpaste to fishing tackle lined the walls. Wicker baskets hung low from the ceiling. Nothing resembled a detective gadget or anything to do with sleuthing.

"Welcome to Mycroft's Mercantile," a woman's voice called from somewhere in the crammed shop.

They had some difficulty finding the woman amidst all the merchandise. Eventually they located her in the back of the shop behind an equally full counter. The children nearly breathed a sigh of relief upon finding her, for they had begun to worry they might be lost in the labyrinth of merchandise.

The woman turned out to be younger than she sounded. She looked to be only about eighteen. She was plump and plain with blue eyes exaggerated by purple eye shadow. Her mouth of crooked teeth chewed gum. She wore a green apron with *Jane* embroidered at the top.

"Whotcha lookin' for?" She chomped on her gum, looking at each customer in turn.

"We're looking for . . ." Mr. Wilson turned to his son. "What exactly do you need, Rollie?"

Rollie hesitated and swept his eyes around the store. Behind the counter were reams of ribbons and spools of thread in every color. To the right of the counter were stacks of used books and baskets of golf balls and matchbooks. To the left were shelves of toiletries. He glanced down into the glass cabinet under the counter. A variety of pastel-colored perfume bottles sparkled. The countertop boasted a few jars of homemade jam and a few glass canisters of red-and-white-striped peppermint sticks. He started to doubt they were in the right shop.

"This is Mycroft's Mercantile, right?" he asked Jane.

She nodded with a slight roll of her eyes. "Do you need somethin' or not?"

"I'm not sure you have what we need," Rollie mumbled. "We need a special solution for invisible ink."

Jane stopped chewing her gum mid-chomp. "Why didn't you say so sooner? You're not gonna find whotcha need in this part of the shop." She came out from behind the counter and squeezed past them. She maneuvered around a coat rack of berets, a pedestal of teapots, and a stack of boxes labeled *nails*. She stopped at a bare wall with a handwritten sign that said *Please ask for assistance*. A small button, much like a doorbell, was beside the sign.

"My dad can help you," Jane told them with a toss of her head. "Which school are you from?"

"We go to Sherlock Academy of Fine Sleuths," Eliot blurted. "It's right around the corner."

"I know the school. The Academy is our biggest client—so is the Marple Institute." Jane pushed the button. "You'll find whotcha need down below."

With a groaning creak of wood, the floorboards beside the bare wall suddenly gave way to a narrow staircase. A runner rug unrolled itself down the stairs, carpeting each step. A soft glow of light shown up from below.

With wide eyes, Mr. Wilson said, "You children go find what you need. I'll look around for Mum's sewing needles."

Rollie led his friends single-file downstairs. The temperature dropped a bit and the air grew damp and musty. The basement was just as small and crammed as the upstairs shop, but instead of random household items, interesting gadgets filled the shelves and counters.

Eliot immediately found a bookshelf lined with all kinds of books on codes, ciphers, and decryptions. Cecily checked out a shelf of different-sized notebooks and journals. Rollie and Wesley headed to the counter, bypassing racks of costumes, stacks of investigation kits, and collections of chemistry supplies.

A brown basset hound sprawled next to the counter. He lifted his head and turned his sleepy eyes to them. He wagged his tail and struggled out a lonely bay.

"Toby, move out of the way," a portly man mumbled.

The man was perched on a stool behind the counter displaying spyglasses and magnifying glasses of different sizes and prices. The middle-aged man wore a yellow cardigan with leather elbow patches. His teeth clamped down on a slender pipe. His head was round, his face was full, his neck was thick, and his shoulders were broad. He had a jolly belly. With his chubby fingers, he sorted through a carton of small pocketknives. As the two boys approached him, his lazy eyes looked up.

"May I help you, lads?" he asked in a deep voice.

Wesley spoke up first. "Yes, sir. We need to purchase a solution for invisible ink."

"And what would two lads like yourself need with an item like that?" He studied them closely and puffed on his pipe.

"We're students from Sherlock Academy," Rollie told him. "We're on a case."

"Ah, that makes more sense. And how do I know you're going to use this solution for a case and not for your own mischief?" he questioned.

Rollie showed him the business card. "Our teacher Mr. Chad gave us your contact information in case we needed anything."

"That seems plausible. Perhaps I should ring Mr. Chad to confirm your story."

"I'm afraid you can't, sir." Rollie groaned. "The Academy's phone lines have been down."

The man scratched his chubby cheek, and smiled. "Right you are, lad. May I have your names just in case I need to check up on you?"

"I'm Wesley Livingston."

"I'm Rollie Wilson."

"Wilson did you say? You wouldn't happen to be a relation of Lady Eileen Wilson, would you?"

"She's my great-aunt."

"That makes all the difference in the world, Rollie Wilson. Welcome to Mycroft's Mercantile. I am Mr. Holmes."

The Other Mr. Holmes

"**D**id you say your name is Mr. Holmes?" Wesley gasped.

"You're related to Sherlock Holmes?" asked Rollie.

"I'm Bartholomew Holmes." He chortled at their enthusiasm. "My father Winston was Sherlock and Mycroft's second cousin. That would make me their third cousin. Since neither of them ever married or had children, the Holmes name has almost died off. My daughter and I are the last, I believe."

"Why did you name the store after Sherlock's brother, Mycroft?" Wesley wanted to know.

"His name is a little more discreet. There are certain parties that are better off not knowing about this little shop of detective tools—or rather we're better off with them not knowing. Sherlock has received enough honor with the Academy. I thought it only right that his brother get some public mention. He was just as brilliant, if not more so, than Sherlock."

"But he was lazy," Rollie said flatly. "He didn't have the ambition Sherlock had."

Mr. Holmes gave a lopsided grin. "Right you are, but he did help Sherlock in some dire situations. You'll remember Mycroft gave Sherlock money and watched over the Baker Street rooms after Sherlock faked his death and hid abroad."

Wesley nodded. "Mycroft was the only person who knew Sherlock had survived his fight with Moriarty."

"And he guarded that knowledge well—he was a good secret keeper." Mr. Holmes winked. "Now Mr. Chad told me a group of students might be dropping by for supplies. He mentioned Rollie Wilson would be leading the group. You need invisible ink solution, did you say?" He turned to a row of little apothecary drawers behind him. "There are many different types of inks and many different types of solutions for them." He opened a few small drawers.

"We're not sure what kind of ink it is," said Rollie. "It smells funny."

"Like vinegar," added Wesley.

Mr. Holmes nodded knowingly. "There is a vinegar-based ink used commonly." He held up a tiny bottle of bright fuchsia liquid. "Extract of red cabbage is the solution for it."

"We need a lot of it," Rollie said, frowning at the little bottle that was no bigger than his thumb. "We need enough to wipe walls with."

Raising his eyebrows in surprise, Mr. Holmes asked, "An invisible message is written on the walls? That's highly unusual. I know what you need." He opened another drawer and brought out a tin canister with a label that read *Magic Red Cabbage Solution for Invisible Ink.* He set it on the counter. "This solution is in powdered form. Mix a tablespoon for every cup of water. I would say for one wall you'll need about two cups. Tell me, who would write on the walls with invisible ink? Did a toddler spy scribble on the walls?" The middle-aged man chuckled.

"Our school's enemy left a list," Wesley explained vaguely.

"Herr Zilch," Mr. Bartholomew Holmes said plainly. "I am very aware of him and his vendetta against the Academy. You lads are brave to work on a case involving MUS. I support anyone willing to stop Zilch. Here's your solution free of charge. Consider it my donation to the cause against MUS."

"Thank you, Mr. Holmes!" the two boys chimed.

"Anything for a Wilson. You must be very proud to be related to Lady Wilson."

Rollie grimaced. He used to feel proud, but not anymore. He felt confused and uneasy. Most of all, he felt angry. Instead of voicing all this, he replied, "Sometimes I forget who she is to other people. She's always just been my great-aunt."

"She's done a whole lot of good in the name of Sherlock Holmes. I hope someday you will do as much," Mr. Holmes admonished. "Tell me, has anyone approached you about joining the Holmes Brigade? You're perfect candidates if you're already working against MUS."

"We're dying to know more about it!" said Wesley.

"Our bodyguard, Euston Hood, is a member, but he says he can't tell us a lot," added Rollie.

"Ah, yes, Mr. Hood is a very secretive soul. What has he told you?"

"He says the Brigade was set up to stop MUS. He says there are always only four members, and he wears a leather wristband with a symbol."

"That is true." Mr. Holmes nodded solemnly. "The symbol represents the Sign of the Four. In this case, the Four are the Brigade members with unique abilities. Every Holmes Brigade is directed by an advisor—a former Brigade member. I know Mr. Hood wants to be an advisor to a new Brigade. Not just anyone can join. You have to be invited to join, and you should consider it seriously before accepting, for it's quite a dangerous position to be a member of the Holmes Brigade. You become a prime target of Herr Zilch."

"We're already targets," muttered Wesley.

"That is why I wondered if you were already members. Perhaps you will be invited soon." Mr. Holmes puffed on his pipe.

"How do *you* know about the Holmes Brigade, sir?" Rollie had to ask.

"Hmm, I was waiting for that question. I am the official Brigade archivist. That is all you need to know at this point."

At that moment, Eliot and Cecily joined the boys at the counter. Eliot grappled with several heavy books while Cecily laid a thick journal on the counter.

"I wish I had known about this shop before Christmas," said Cecily. "I would have put some items on my wish list. How much is this journal, sir?"

"Five pounds and fifty-p."

"Oh dear, that's more than I have with me today." Cecily's face fell with disappointment. She was about to put the journal back when Mr.

Holmes took it from her and slipped it into a paper bag.

"I'll just put it on your tab. Mr. Chad set up a tab for you. He figured you would need supplies now and then."

"In that case," Eliot butted in, dropping the four heavy books on the counter, "I'll take these. I really could have used them to crack that code last night. I'll have to get other book jackets to cover these."

His friends read the titles on the spines: *Code Collections, A Complete Guide to Common Code Algorithms, Decoding Made Easy,* and *What's Your Cypher?*

Rollie smiled at Cecily. "Don't you have enough notebooks?"

Cecily smiled back. "You can never have too many. Besides, this one reminds me of Zilch's journal—it's the same size and paper quality. I'm feeling inspired to keep a diary of my secret life as a detective."

"Rollie!" Mr. Wilson called from upstairs. "Are you about finished?"

"Coming, Dad! Thank you again, Mr. Holmes." Rollie shook the man's large, beefy hand. "I'm sure we'll be back."

"I'm sure you will. Next time, you can come directly here from the school." Mr. Holmes jerked his thumb at a closed red door by the counter. "Through that door is a direct tunnel to the Academy."

"The secret passage leads here?" Rollie gasped excitedly.

Mr. Holmes smiled. "That secret passage, as you call it, leads many places. Ask your great-aunt more about it."

On the car ride home, Rollie and Wesley explained to Mr. Wilson, Cecily, and Eliot Mr. Holmes's relation to their favorite detective. Cecily was excited to know that the shop owner was a Mr. Holmes, while Eliot remained skeptical as to Mr. Holmes' identity. He did not recall ever reading about any of Sherlock's relations besides Mycroft.

Back at the Wilson manor, Rollie and his friends gathered in his room to spell out their plan.

"We'll need a bowl and paintbrush," Wesley said. "And a measuring cup and tablespoon."

"We've got all that in the kitchen," Rollie replied.

Cecily giggled with anticipation. "So what are we waiting for?"

"Euston!" Rollie and Wesley groaned together.

"Is Eliot up for distracting him again?" Cecily turned to the boy who stood with arms crossed defiantly.

"Not Eliot." Wesley shook his head. "We'll need him. I've got an idea. Let's use Uncle Ky to distract him."

They filed downstairs to find Uncle Ky. They found him humming as usual and back to work on the puzzle in the parlor. They quickly laid out Wesley's plan to him.

"Let me see," Uncle Ky said with a glimmer of intrigue beneath his bushy eyebrows. "You need me to engage in a conversation with this Hood character, eh? That is a tall order, or have you not noticed how quiet the man is?"

"I know he is," Rollie told his great-uncle. "You don't need to make him talk. You just have to make him stay and listen to *you* talk. Tell him about all your careers."

"I can do that. Leave it to me, detectives." Uncle Ky gave them a thumbs-up. "Where is he?"

"We'll get him," Rollie said as he and his friends hurried into their winter coats.

It took them awhile to locate Euston, for he was constantly roving around the property checking on things. They finally found him walking up the street from the corner. They convinced Euston that Uncle Ky needed to speak with him immediately and watched him enter the Wilson house.

The sleuths hurried around the snow forts they had built and over to the tall brick wall separating the Wilson's back garden from Zilch's. They mounted the bare mulberry tree learning against the wall. With the help of a sturdy limb, they climbed over the brick wall and landed in Zilch's garden. They ran to the cellar window and dropped through.

Wasting no time, they rushed upstairs to the study. From a brown paper bag, Rollie dumped out a large paintbrush, small bowl, measuring cup, tablespoon, and the tin can of *Magic Red* solution. He took the bowl and measuring cup to a nearby bathroom. From the tap, he measured and poured four cups of cold water into the bowl. When he returned to the study, he found Cecily had opened the can of solution and was waiting with the first tablespoon.

"Four tablespoons, right?" she asked.

Rollie set the bowl of water on the floor next to her. She carefully scooped out and dropped four tablespoons of powdered solution into the water bowl. She stirred it around until the fuchsia powder dissolved.

"Start with this wall." Wesley tapped an unpainted wall near the door.

"Get ready to copy down the list," Rollie told his friends. "I'm sure this is it!"

He dipped the paintbrush into the bowl of fuchsia solution. He swept the paintbrush over the wall. Everyone waited breathlessly to see what would happen.

Nothing—at first.

Then, gradually, silvery letters appeared on the wall.

"Quick! Write it down!" Rollie yelled.

Cecily and Eliot both copied down the words in their pocket notepads.

"It's an address!" Wesley gasped excitedly. "This is it! The MUS list!"

Rollie continued painting the wall, revealing a long list of names that reached to the floor.

"I can't reach any higher," Rollie said, stretching up on his tiptoes.

Wesley knelt and gave Rollie a boost. Rollie wiped clear up to the ceiling; nothing else appeared. He dipped the brush into the last of the solution and tackled the last unpainted wall. Right in the middle, at his eye level, another address with a long list of names below it appeared down to the floor. Cecily and Eliot scribbled the list down.

"Quick! The solution is drying—the names are fading!" Wesley urged.

"We're writing as fast as we can!" snapped Eliot.

Rollie stood back from the wall. "That's it. I wish these other two walls hadn't been painted over."

"You did it, Rollie!" Cecily hugged her friend.

Rollie did not mind her affection, though if his brothers got wind of their embrace, he would never hear the end of it. "*We* did it! We found the MUS list. I knew we were onto it."

"Let's get this to Headmaster right away," Wesley said.

"Wait, I want to leave a message for Zilch." Rollie fished out his pocket notepad from his back trouser pocket.

Eliot looked worried. "What message?"

"I've been thinking a lot about this," Rollie answered. "We should meet his challenge."

"Are you bonkers, Rollie?" Cecily gaped at him. "He's dangerous!"

"It's too risky messing with him," Wesley agreed.

"It's worth the risk," Rollie insisted.

Eliot eyed him. "What's your plan? You need a plan before you just rush into this."

"We'll leave a note for the secretary to take to him. She'll definitely return tonight. We'll challenge Zilch to come. It's the only way to catch him, don't you see?"

Wesley looked puzzled. "Why do we need to catch him? We have the list. Headmaster and Scotland Yard can track him down."

"We have two parts of the list, but there are four walls. The secretary has already covered the other two parts." Rollie waved his hand at the painted walls. "This list will help track down his agents, but it may not lead us to him. This could be our chance to catch Zilch!"

"You plan to get Headmaster's help, right?" Cecily asked. "And Scotland Yard's help?"

"Absolutely! We also have Euston." Rollie quickly scribbled down a message in his notepad. He ripped out the page and read the message aloud.

"Herr Zilch: We have your journal and we are willing to return it to you. We do not scare off easily, so don't bother with any more threats. Let's see if you mean what you say. Signed, The Holmes Brigade."

"That will make him mad," Wesley mumbled. "We had better make sure Headmaster and Scotland Yard can be here with us if he shows up."

"Let's wait and see if he responds to us." Rollie folded the message and left it on the windowsill.

"We can't give him back that journal!" squealed Cecily. "We haven't read it all yet."

"We have to offer the journal—it's the only bait we've got," Rollie reasoned. "We'll get the journal back when we capture him."

"What if we don't capture him?"

Rollie's jaw clenched. "We will this time. Let me see those addresses and names."

Cecily handed her notepad to him.

"This first address is in Brighton. That's where you live, right, Wesley? It's 28 Old Shoreham Road. Do you know where that is?"

Wesley's eyes widened. "I know where Old Shoreham Road is, but I'm not sure where number 28 is. It's a long road with tons of little shops and flats."

Rollie skimmed the list of five names below the address. "A.B. Torin, L.L. Wilsh, P.O. Carter— these must be agents at the Brighton headquarters." He read the second address. "This one's in Dublin.

Number 28 Drury Street. I didn't know MUS was active in Ireland also. There are eight agents listed here. We must get this list to Headmaster. In the meantime, we've got a lot to do."

Once they were back at the Wilsons, they dispersed to do their pre-assigned errands. Cecily went to tell Uncle Ky he could stop chatting to Euston, who looked nearly blue in the face. She and Eliot caught Euston up on what they had discovered. Rollie and Wesley tried to phone Sherlock Academy.

"Their phones must still be down," Rollie groaned. "I'm not getting through. Why's it taking so long to get the phone service working again?"

"Must be all this freak snow. We should take the list to him then," Wesley suggested. "Euston could take us."

"Rollie!" Eliot hollered from the entry hall. "You'll never guess who's here!"

The boys raced to join Eliot and Cecily at the front door. They smiled at the tall woman standing stiffly before them. Her brown hair was pulled back tightly in a bun, and her crisp, tan coat was buttoned up to her chin.

Ms. Katherine Yardsly nodded in greeting. "Good afternoon, students. Headmaster sent me to check on you and get a report from Mr. Hood. Our phones are still disconnected."

"We were just trying to get ahold of Headmaster." Quickly, Rollie, with the help of his comrades, told Ms. Yardsly all about their investigations and new discovery.

Cecily and Eliot passed their notepads to their teacher.

Ms. Yardsly took them, read the list of addresses and names, and gave a tight smile. "Well done, sleuths! I will take this to Headmaster Yardsly immediately. We will keep you informed." In her militant style, she spun on her heel and marched outside. After exchanging a few words with Euston, she climbed into a waiting hansom and departed down the street.

Euston poked his head through the front door. "I must commend you on your findings, but I must also warn you not to leave the premises again. Your safety is at stake. Understand?"

"Yes, sir," the four chimed.

As the front door closed, Rollie turned to Cecily. "Thank you for not mentioning my challenge to Zilch."

"It wasn't mine to mention. This is your plan, Rollie. But I would like you to know I'm not entirely comfortable with it. What if something happens to you?"

"Don't worry. If Zilch writes back saying he'll come, we'll definitely tell Euston. We'll need his help getting Scotland Yard and Headmaster."

"Are you hoping Zilch will come?" asked Eliot.

"Yes, for everyone else's sake. We need to catch him. But I have to be honest; I am afraid."

Whistle Blowing

"I knew he'd write back." Rollie fingered the envelope. It was the next morning after breakfast. After another sneaky escapade while Euston used the bathroom, the sleuths managed to retrieve the letter left by Zilch's secretary the night before. They gathered in Rollie's room, waiting to read what Herr Zilch's answer would be to their threat.

"Open it already!" urged Eliot.

Rollie tore open the envelope. He felt anxious to read Zilch's response but also hesitant to face the future. He pulled out a single slip of paper. He read it to himself then passed it to Cecily.

She took it and read it aloud.

"Holmes Brigade,

You leave me no choice but to agree to a meeting. My conditions are simple but nonnegotiable. First, I will meet with Rollin only. I have no interest in Cecily Brighton and Eliot Tildon. Rollin, if you would feel safer having Wesley Livingston along as your lookout, I have no objections. He can watch outside if you like, but he must not partake in our meeting. Second, you must bring my journal that you stole. I will meet you in my old study at noon tomorrow.

Herr Zilch."

"How does he know my name?" Eliot shrieked. "Who told?"

"Now he's really scaring me," Cecily said.

"I told you not to underestimate him." Wesley shook his head. "Did he say noon? It's ten-thirty now. Why noon? I'd expect he'd want to meet under cover by night."

Rollie took a deep breath. "Wesley, will you be my lookout?"

"Absolutely! I'll guard the cellar window and make sure none of Zilch's cronies follow after you. We should have a signal in case something goes wrong."

"That's a good idea. We can use my bobby whistles Uncle Ky gave me. Cecily and Eliot, you'll hitch a ride with my parents into town when they take Uncle Ky to the station. His train leaves at noon." Rollie paused. "You don't think Zilch wants to meet at noon because he knows my family will be gone, do you?"

Panic filled Cecily's green eyes. "Now he's *really* scaring me!"

"Just a coincidence," Eliot murmured in a weak voice.

"There are no such things as coincidences when crimes are afoot," Wesley said. "Holmes says so."

Rollie continued with the plan. "The phones are still down at the Academy. So Cecily, Eliot, my parents will drop you off at school and you'll get Headmaster."

"Are we asking Euston for help?" Cecily asked.

Rollie nodded. "We need to tell him what's going on. He needs to go fetch Scotland Yard."

"If I know Euston, he won't leave you to meet with Zilch alone," Wesley warned.

"We can't tell him we're meeting with Zilch," Rollie said. "We'll just tell him we think Zilch will show up. We'll offer to stay here and watch out for him. That's not a total lie."

Cecily gave him a motherly look. "It's close."

"It's the only way to catch Zilch." Rollie's middle fluttered with the thought of skewing the truth. "The most important part of this whole plan is Headmaster and Scotland Yard must arrive here just in time. If they're here before noon, they'll scare off Zilch. If they wait too long . . . " He trailed off, not wanting to think about all the possible dangerous things that could happen being left alone with Zilch for too long.

"We'll be sure to tell Headmaster about the timing," Eliot assured him.

"I would just like to remind everyone that I don't like this plan." Cecily crossed her arms. "I don't like leaving Rollie alone to face Zilch, and I don't think it's a good idea to give him back his journal. Isn't there another way?"

"Maybe, but I think this could be our best chance at catching Zilch," said Rollie. "And we'll get the journal back when we catch him. You guys go talk to Euston."

The group split up. Rollie glanced out his bedroom window at the vacant house next door. He had known he would have to face Herr Zilch again. He just had not counted on it being this soon. He knew the risk was worthwhile to catch the villain.

He was just not too thrilled about taking the risk. In the past, his skills and courage had aided him in solving mysteries and thwarting Zilch's plans. But this time was different. This time he did not have Auntie Ei's backing.

He fished out Auntie Ei's letters from his hollow Shakespeare book. He unfolded one letter and read it.

By no means accept my great-nephew Rollin under the circumstances we discussed. I do not wish him to receive special privileges because of who I am and who he will be.

He knew no good would come of reading these letters again, especially now, on the brink of a face-off with his enemy. Still, he could not help himself. He read one more.

I would prefer he be expelled rather than accepted under the circumstances.

He was not sure how his courage would hold up, especially when meeting Zilch face-to-face. The last time Rollie had met Zilch, the villain had nearly kidnapped him.

He wondered if Holmes had felt this way right before he had faced Professor Moriarty and dueled to the death. He wondered if Holmes had been anxious about the outcome of their meeting or if he had been hesitant to face his nemesis once and for all. He wondered if Holmes had been afraid.

Suddenly, Rollie remembered his pledge to stop Herr Zilch no matter the cost.

Today the cost was his safety—perhaps even his life, but he was willing to pay the cost for the good of everyone else and for the good of Sherlock Academy. He had a feeling that was exactly what Holmes had considered as he hiked up Reichenbach Falls and waited for Moriarty to meet him. Holmes had considered the cost and was willing to pay it.

Rollie took heart from Holmes. He just hoped he would be strong enough.

*　*　*　*

Rollie poked his head into the guest room. Uncle Ky was all flustered as he gathered his belongings and crammed them into his suitcase. His visit had been cut short by a telegram announcing a hurriedly called staff meeting in Oxford that he was required to attend. He was not at all pleased with having to go so soon. Rollie thought this was suspicious.

"Perhaps this is my signal to retire from this position," Uncle Ky muttered as he found his scarf underneath the bed. "I've been at it for nearly a year now, you know. That is a significant amount of time for someone like me."

Rollie smiled. "I hope you have a safe journey home. My parents and Auntie Ei are taking you to Paddington station, right?"

"Yes. I always require Eileen to send me off. It's the least she can do for a brother she sees but once a year. Good-bye, Rollin. I wish you the best in your studies and your cases. Remember, don't let people define you. If anything's going to define you, it should be your strong character and your moral convictions. And of course any little hobbies you care to indulge in." With a wink, Uncle Ky picked up his bulging suitcase and departed downstairs.

Once they got to the entry hall, everyone pulled on their heavy coats. Auntie Ei seemed rather annoyed at having to go out into the snowy city to take her brother to Paddington Station. Mr. Wilson was already outside warming up the automobile. Cecily and Eliot gave Rollie reassuring squeezes and pats.

"Zilch's journal is on your desk," Cecily said on her way out the door.

"We'll be gone just a few hours. We're going to do a little shopping near Hyde Park after dropping off Uncle Ky," Mrs. Wilson told her son. "Ed and Stew are working. Lucille and Daphne are at Noelle's house down the street. I understand Euston has left on an errand, so you and Wesley will be here alone. Don't get into trouble." She kissed the top of his sandy-blond head and closed the front door behind her.

"Wesley!" Rollie hurried up to his room where he found his friend spying through the binoculars. "We still have a half hour to go. Do you think we should go over there early so I'm there first?"

Wesley thought for a moment. "It would probably be the smartest thing to do. That way you can make sure Zilch doesn't hide his agents in the house beforehand. I'll guard the cellar window, of course. I can whistle when I spot him coming." He slipped one of the silver policeman whistles into his front trouser pocket.

Rollie took the other one and snatched up Zilch's journal. He and Wesley traipsed downstairs to the entry hall and dressed for the snow. Without a word, the two boys headed over to Zilch's vacant house. Before Rollie hopped through the cellar window, Wesley stopped him.

"Be careful—you mean a lot to us," he told Rollie. "Besides, if it wasn't for you, I would still be working for Zilch without knowing it. And we wouldn't be about to catch him now. Holmes has always been my hero, but you know what? I think you might be my new Holmes."

Rollie smiled. "You're a good friend and good comrade, Wesley Livingston. I'm glad you've got my back today."

"And I'm glad you've got *my* back, Rollie Wilson."

The boys shook hands solidly. Then Rollie hopped through the window, leaving Wesley outside to guard. He was relieved to find the upstairs study empty. With a little difficulty, he pried open the window, so he and Wesley could hear each other's whistles more clearly. He paced the small room, stopping every so often to peer out the window.

He wondered what he and Zilch would discuss. He hoped that help would arrive on time. He did not have a watch, so he had no idea what time it was. It seemed like he had been there forever, but it probably had been only about ten minutes.

His middle fluttered, his heart pounded, and his palms sweated. He tore off his mittens. Of all the daring escapades he had done in the past, this was by far the most dangerous. He felt the most—

Tweet! Tweet!

Rollie stiffened. That was Wesley's signal.

Herr Zilch had arrived.

Up on the House

Rollie planted his feet in the center of the room. He gripped the leather-bound journal and ran his fingers across the branded name on the cover: *F. A. Zilch*. He trained his eyes on the door and clenched his jaw. He heard the front door open. Euston must have forgotten to lock up after the last time he escorted Rollie and Wesley back home. The door slammed closed.

Thud, thud, thud.

Rollie heard slow but steady footsteps climb the stairs one at a time. And before he had any more time to let the reality of what was happening sink in . . .

Herr Zilch was there.

The man and the boy regarded one another. It had been about two months since they had seen each other in person, and even then Zilch had been disguised as Professor Enches. Rollie had never seen Zilch's true self, for he had also been in disguise when he had been the neighbor Mr. Crenshaw. For the first time, Rollie saw Zilch's true appearance, or at least he assumed it was.

Herr Zilch was thinner than Rollie remembered. Fine wrinkles lined his beady eyes, and Rollie guessed he had to be nearing his seventies. He had sprouted a very neat mustache that distinguished him a bit. He wore a long gray wool coat and black leather gloves. A smart fedora hid his silver hair. Rollie was surprised to see Zilch carrying Watson's Case. Zilch barely glanced at Rollie as he appraised the room.

"Ah, it's good to be home." He gave a sardonic smile. "This was always my favorite room in the house. It's small and cozy, and from that window, I had an excellent view of *your* house. I see Scotland Yard has confiscated everything here in my study . . . they did not leave so much as a match."

Rollie licked his lips.

"You're taller, my boy," Herr Zilch said in a soft voice. "I suppose that's what happens when you turn another year older. You are twelve now, correct?"

Rollie nodded, slightly taken aback by Zilch's conversational inquiries. "Take off your gloves. Show me your hands. Prove that you're Frederick Zilch."

Zilch smiled thinly beneath his mustache. "A smart move, lad." He stripped his gloves to reveal his horribly scarred hands. "It appears these days you are growing into quite the detective. Your great-aunt must be very proud. You are turning out to be exactly who she planned you to be." He pulled his gloves back on.

Rollie frowned. He remembered what he had read in one of Auntie Ei's letters: *I do not wish him to receive special privileges because of who I am and who he will be.*

"Speaking of Eileen, I have some personal items to return to her," Zilch continued, flinging Watson's Case across the room.

The small metal lock box landed at Rollie's feet and sprang open, spilling white lacy undergarments on the floor. Rollie couldn't hide his smile, for he still thought swapping Watson's manuscripts for Auntie Ei's underwear had been one of his more clever ideas.

Zilch scowled. "Surely you must know that if it weren't for your Aunt Eileen, you would never have attended Sherlock Academy or begun your journey as a detective. Tell me, would you have chosen to be a detective otherwise? Even after my threat?"

Zilch took a few steps nearer, and a few more. He began to slowly pace around Rollie.

Rollie swallowed. This was not how he envisioned the conversation going.

Had he been letting Auntie Ei define him? If not for her, he would never have known anything about Sherlock Holmes and would not have attended the Academy. He would not be standing in this tiny room with this dangerous man if it were not for her influence on him.

After reading those letters between Auntie Ei and Yardsly, he now wondered if her encouragement had been sincere. It seemed there had been a time when she did not want him to be detective. Had her encouragement been a lie?

"I've been wondering if she put you up to meeting me today." Zilch paced some more, very slowly and in control. "Is she still manipulating you?"

Rollie's eyes flashed. "No, she did not put me up to this. She doesn't even know I'm meeting you. This was my choice!"

Zilch stopped and studied him, the faintest traces of surprise on his face.

"You've been manipulated, too," Rollie said, his voice finding strength. "Maybe not by another person, but you've been manipulated by your regrets and fears. I know all about you."

Zilch's eyes darted to his wristwatch. "I gather you've been talking with my nephew."

Rollie's brow furrowed. "I read your journal."

For the briefest moment, a hint of panic flashed in Zilch's beady eyes. It was there and gone almost too fast to notice, but Rollie caught it.

"You have it with you?" asked Zilch.

Rollie held the journal up in his hand.

Zilch nodded curtly. "Did you find my attaché case under the floorboards? I intended you to find it." He stomped his boot on the floor. "My secretary planted it during her first visit."

"You wanted me to find that?" Rollie cocked his head to one side. "Why?"

"You should not be so quick to join the Holmes Brigade. Those photographs in the case are former Brigaders. I have eliminated all but a few of those members, and I will not hesitate to eliminate any future Brigaders." Zilch looked pointedly at Rollie. He closed the study door.

Rollie took a deep breath as panic made his middle flutter. "You're afraid of me. You're afraid of what I might become."

"You are a boy!" Zilch's face heated. "I do not fear you! I didn't even bring a weapon today! I want you to know what you're getting yourself into before pursuing this path Eileen has set you on. My nephew did not know what he was getting himself into when he betrayed me. I am sure he has shared his regrets with you."

Rollie wracked his brain to make sense of Zilch's implications. Zilch knew, or at least suspected, that Rollie had contact with his nephew.

Rollie, stalling for time, decided to get a few things cleared up while he had the chance. "Were you a Brigade member?"

Zilch's mustache twitched. "I do not see the necessity of shedding any light on the past for you. Ask your Aunt Eileen about that."

Rollie rolled his eyes in frustration but continued with his next question. "Why did your secretary return to paint over the MUS list? Why now? The house has been vacant since you fled five months ago."

He glanced out the window, watching for help to come. He hoped Cecily and Eliot had found Yardsly.

"My house has been under constant surveillance by Scotland Yard since August. Just two weeks ago, the Yard called off the surveillance. I suppose they've found better things to do. I jumped at the opportunity to dispose of my list. I had not had time to do so in August before I left. I wanted my secretary to paint all the walls quickly, but she worked so slowly. She managed to copy and destroy half the list. I assume you have the other half?" Zilch tipped his hat at Rollie.

"Why did you write your list on the walls instead of on paper?"

Zilch smirked. "Never leave a paper trail. I learned that lesson the hard way when you intercepted my letters to Enches."

"You can have your journal, but first I want to know something else."

Herr Zilch glanced at his wristwatch. "My time is precious. What is your question?"

"Why did you want to kidnap Wesley? He doesn't know anything about you or MUS. He has no secrets to betray."

Zilch paused. "I have my reasons. All you must know is that I will not hesitate to do anything that gives me the upper hand in this game. I warned you to know what you're getting yourself into by fighting me and joining the Holmes Brigade." Crossing his arms, he steadily circled Rollie.

"I know what I'm getting into," Rollie said firmly. "I've chosen to be a detective, and I'm going to stop you." He glanced quickly out the window again when he thought he heard a car.

"You're more stubborn than I anticipated, but your nerve is only as strong as your comrades. I doubt you would be so bold if your auntie failed to support you."

Did he know something about that? Did he know the reason Auntie Ei had not wanted him to be a detective at first?

"And I doubt you would be so bold without your comrades—what are their names again? Ah yes, I remember." He whipped out three wallet-size photographs and held them up. "Eliot Tildon, Cecily Brighton, and, of course, Wesley Livingston."

Rollie recognized his friends' faces in the photographs. They had red X's over them. How did he—

"Yes, I know who they are, boy. Professor Enches discovered more about you and them than you thought. While kidnapping Wesley failed, my message did not. Beware, I will not hesitate to eliminate anyone in my way, especially if they're your accomplices and members of the Holmes Brigade. You may add these to that collection of photographs in the attaché case."

Slowly, deliberately, Zilch tore each photograph in half. He tossed the shreds at Rollie's feet.

Rollie's stomach churned. He slipped his hand into his pocket and squeezed the whistle for reassurance.

"And when you are alone, your courage will be reduced to nothing, and you will realize you were never a real detective." Zilch edged nearer until he was so close Rollie could smell tobacco on his breath. "You are nothing more than the expectations of your family and friends. You have no hope of stopping me or my plans."

Rollie gulped. He tried to imagine life without his friends and family. He imagined being alone, working on a case alone, and fighting Herr Zilch alone. And he felt small. Maybe Zilch was right. Maybe he was not really a detective but was just acting the part everyone wanted him to play. He was just a boy.

"Did you also find the file I left about the Final Problem?" Zilch stepped back and checked his watch. "Under the bricks?" He jerked his head at the little fireplace.

Rollie nodded and checked the window.

"Good. You no doubt gathered it refers to my final plan to destroy you, the Holmes Brigade, and, most importantly, Sherlock Academy of Fine Sleuths. I am afraid there is not much you can do to stop it from happening. If you agree to walk away from the Brigade and your absurd mission to stop me, you have my word I won't harm you or your family and friends." Zilch held out a gloved hand.

Rollie glanced at it. He had no idea what the Final Problem was, but for the moment, he doubted he could stop it, especially if he were all alone. What would Zilch do to Cecily and Eliot and Wesley? What would he do to his dad and mum and siblings and Auntie Ei? Was being a detective worth risking their safety? Did he even have a right to call himself a detective?

He no longer felt sure about anything.

"You are wise to consider my offer," Herr Zilch said quietly. "Sherlock Holmes should have been so wise. He was a fool to challenge Professor Moriarty."

Hearing that name—Sherlock Holmes—awakened new feelings in Rollie, including a little bit of courage.

He cleared his throat. "Not true—Moriarty was a fool to challenge Sherlock Holmes. Holmes defeated him at Reichenbach Falls."

Herr Zilch's face reddened. "Moriarty's sacrifice was necessary. It spurred on his comrades to form MUS."

Rollie would not back down. "Moriarty's death wasn't a sacrifice. It was his failure. He meant to kill Holmes but couldn't. There was nothing noble about Moriarty's death!"

"You should not trick yourself into thinking you are anything like Sherlock Holmes. You will only delude yourself by thinking you can stop me. Sherlock Holmes may have eliminated Moriarty, but in doing so, he strengthened MUS. *He* was the ultimate failure."

"No, MUS couldn't accept that Holmes had won. You should know that you won't win either."

"That is still to be decided."

Zilch grabbed Rollie's collar and pushed the boy into a corner of the room. He gripped the boy's coat collar and glared down at him. "You are nothing more than a pawn in this game. *They* are using you. You're just a boy. You are *not* Sherlock Holmes."

Rollie took a deep breath. He expected that comment to stab him deep. But it did not . . . and that was when Rollie knew who he was.

"You're right. I am not Sherlock Holmes."

Zilch nodded.

"I am Rollie Wilson, the detective who will defeat you!"

Zilch pinned him against the wall. Rollie did not break eye contact. Zilch released his grip on Rollie's collar and stepped back.

"Very well, my little adversary. You have chosen your path. I have warned you of the consequences. My journal, if you please."

Rollie handed it to him. Zilch took out a silver lighter from his outer coat pocket. He flicked the lighter on and held the small blue flame up to the corner of his journal.

"NO!" Rollie yelled. "Why are you destroying it?"

"Like I've said, never leave a paper trail."

Rollie watched in horror as the journal caught fire, its leather cover shriveling and its pages crinkling in the flames. Zilch tossed it into the empty fireplace, where it continued to burn.

"There is no more to be said between us. Adieu!"

An extraordinary thing happened next. Zilch suddenly leaned back into the wall, which opened up and swallowed him.

Rollie raced to the window and looked out.

Still no sign of Headmaster Yardsly or Scotland Yard. He had to stall Zilch. He could not let him escape.

Rollie charged through the wall opening and hustled up a narrow, steep staircase. To his surprise, he found himself on the roof of the house. He dodged a few slippery puddles of snow and scoured the rooftop.

Herr Zilch stood on the edge and turned back to see Rollie approaching him.

"Do not follow me! I will not hesitate to take drastic action to ensure my escape."

"No! Not this time!" Rollie neared him.

"What can you possibly do to stop me?"

"Anything I can think of." Having no weapon of any kind, Rollie could only use a distraction to keep Zilch on the roof until help arrived.

Where was everyone?

Rollie stooped down next to a patch of snow. He scooped some up in his bare hands, crunched it into a snowball, and hurled it at Zilch. His aim was perfect; he knocked off the fedora, revealing a receding hairline. The fedora twirled down over the side of the house. Zilch looked both shocked and infuriated.

Rollie made another snowball and chucked it. This time Zilch dodged it.

Down the street, Rollie thought he heard tires screech. He hoped it was the sound of help coming.

Zilch started climbing over the edge of the roof.

That was when Rollie noticed for the first time an iron-wrought ladder much like those on fire escapes.

He dove for Zilch and grabbed his coat sleeve. In response, Zilch grabbed Rollie's coat sleeve and pulled on it. Rollie dropped to his belly, grabbed the ladder for support, and pulled back on Zilch's sleeve. They were locked together.

"Let me go, or I'll pull you over!" Zilch screamed, trying to pry his arm loose from the boy. He took a step down the ladder.

With his bare fingers, Rollie clenched his grip on Zilch's coat sleeve and tried to pull up. Zilch was stronger. He yanked Rollie's sleeve, causing him to slip toward the edge. Only Rollie's legs remained on the roof. Then he heard a few things at once.

He heard tires screech to a halt in the street below.

He heard frantic blasts from a whistle.

And he heard fabric tearing.

His coat sleeve tore free from his arm. Zilch lost his balance, and with a shriek, fell backward off the ladder. Rollie watched in horror as the man fell into the thick snow with a dull thud. He continued to watch in horror as Zilch rolled to his feet, snatched up his fedora, and ran to the street. Zilch then dove into a waiting black automobile that sped off immediately.

Right behind, another black automobile with blaring sirens sped off in hot pursuit.

Rollie lay on his stomach, leaning over the roof-top, cold and shaken, his sleeveless arm hanging over the edge. Zilch had escaped . . . again.

"ROLLIN! Come down from there!"

He glanced down into the snowy front yard and saw Headmaster Yardsly waving up at him. Ms. Yardsly, Auntie Ei, Cecily, and Eliot crowded around him, all looking up at the roof.

Carefully, Rollie squirmed away from the edge. He scrambled to his feet and trudged across the roof. He found the trapdoor leading back inside. When he reached the study, Cecily and Eliot were rushing into the room. Cecily threw her arms around him, and Eliot patted him on the back.

"Are you okay?"

"What were you doing on the roof?"

"Are you hurt?"

"Where's your sleeve?"

"What's that smoke smell from?"

Rollie did not answer their questions that came all at once. He only wanted to talk to one person at the moment. He hurried through the house and out to the porch where the adults were.

"Headmaster! Did you catch Zilch? Did he get away?"

Yardsly rested a hand on his shoulder. "Scotland Yard is chasing after him. Euston is with them. We can only hope for the best now, but something worse has happened."

"What could be worse than Zilch escaping?" Rollie felt his chest tightening with panic.

"They kidnapped Wesley!"

The Holmes Brigade

Rollie's head spun. His middle churned.

"What? How? I thought . . . "

"Two MUS agents snatched him when Zilch fell off the roof," Yardsly explained. "They forced him into the car, and they all sped off."

Rollie held his head in his hands. The whistle, their signal—he had heard it. And suddenly everything made sense.

"That was his plan all along."

"How could he have planned that?" Auntie Ei spoke up.

"Zilch told me to bring Wesley as my lookout. He lured me onto the roof to be out of the way. This is all my fault!"

Ms. Yardsly gripped Rollie's shoulder. "Rollin, this is not your fault! Scotland Yard will find them."

"We will get Wesley back," Headmaster Yardsly agreed. "Especially since we have half of the MUS list. If we move quickly enough, we can at least arrest half of his agents. That's a victory we must not neglect. Let's return to your house, Rollin. I told Euston to call there with a report."

The group returned to the Wilson manor. Rollie's parents were still in town, so he invited everyone into the parlor. He sat on the floor by the fire with Cecily and Eliot. Since he was so distracted with the turn of events, he had forgotten to take off his coat.

Cecily pulled if off his shoulders. "I guess you need a new coat," she muttered, examining the frayed threads that had once held a sleeve together.

"ROLLIN!" Headmaster Yardsly said as he sat down on the sofa. "Tell me about your meeting with Herr Zilch."

Rollie relayed the conversation and the struggle on the rooftop. He did not go into detail about Zilch's opinions of Auntie Ei. He would talk to her about that in private. However, he was sure to tell every detail Zilch had said about the Final Problem.

"This worries me," Headmaster Yardsly admitted. "Not only does the nature of it worry me , but it also worries me that Zilch intentionally wanted us to know about it. WHAT DOES HE MEAN?"

"We have a few months to decipher it," Ms. Yardsly stated calmly. "We should utilize Euston."

"EUSTON! Why hasn't he called yet?" Headmaster leapt up and paced the carpet. "Why did Zilch kidnap Wesley? He doesn't know anything about MUS."

"Wesley thought it was for revenge," said Rollie.

Headmaster shook his head. "That seems too petty. When it comes to Zilch, we must always think deeper and smarter. There is another reason, but I'm not sure what it is."

Ring-ring!

Everyone jumped to his or her feet—even Auntie Ei. Headmaster Yardsly rushed to the telephone by the stairs.

"EUSTON?"

The group waited breathlessly with him.

"WHAT? I see. Very well. Yes, I think that's best. Good-bye." Yardsly hung up the phone and turned to them. "They lost Zilch."

Moans and groans filled the room.

"Scotland Yard nearly caught up to them on Prince Albert Road but got separated by the traffic in Trafalgar Square. MUS boarded a train at Victoria station.

Euston is returning so we can make a better plan. We've had one victory though. We got Zilch's secretary!"

"Finally!" Auntie Ei breathed.

"She was caught trying to board the train at Victoria Station. They're taking her to the Yard for questioning."

"I almost forgot!" cried Rollie. "There's more bad news. Zilch burned his journal."

"WHAT? We needed that journal for clues!" Yardsly ran a hand over his face.

"I'm so sorry, sir! I shouldn't have given it to him. I thought we'd get it back when we arrested him. I didn't think he'd burn it and now—"

"He didn't burn it," Cecily interrupted.

"Yes, he did! He lit it with his lighter and threw it—"

Cecily shook her head. "He burned *a* journal, but not *his* journal."

"What are you talking about?"

Cecily ran over to her coat hanging on the hall tree by the front door. Out of a pocket, she retrieved a cover-less journal. She handed it to Headmaster Yardsly. "I tore it from the leather cover. Rollie, remember that journal I bought from Mycroft's Mercantile? I glued it inside the leather cover. That's what Herr Zilch burned."

Yardsly flipped through the pages and beamed. "WELL DONE!"

Rollie gaped at his comrade. "Why did you do that, and why didn't you tell me?"

"I've learned not to underestimate Zilch. Holmes always said to stay in control of the clues. I thought it was too risky to lose a clue as important as that journal. And I didn't tell you, Rollie, because if Zilch discovered it was a fake, I didn't want you to get in trouble. If you were just as shocked as him to find it was a fake, maybe Zilch wouldn't blame you and you'd be safe. You know I was worried about your safety all along."

Rollie stared at her with admiration. "You're quite brilliant, Watson."

"Thank you, Holmes. Though I have to admit I got the idea to switch the covers from Eliot and his cover-switching."

Eliot pointed a finger at her. "I told you it was a good idea!"

"Sir, we have to get Wesley back—we have to!" Rollie urged.

Yardsly nodded resolutely. "We will. Do not fear. Katherine, I think we had better go next door and search for clues."

Ms. Yardsly followed her brother out of the house.

"Wesley will be okay, won't he?" Cecily asked, her eyes misting over. "They won't hurt him, will they?"

Auntie Ei frowned a deeper frown than usual. "Let us hope for the best. Rollin, I would like a word with you." She led him into the library and closed the door. After seating herself in the armchair, she took a deep breath. "I am proud of you for standing up against Herr Zilch."

Rollie frowned. "Even though you didn't want me to be a detective . . . and you didn't want me to go to the Academy."

"Are you still brooding over that letter you found in my desk?"

"And the ones from you to Headmaster—I found them in my Sherlock Holmes volume in the secret library. I don't understand!"

Auntie Ei sighed. "I have always wanted you to go to the Academy and be a great detective, but I wanted those things for you only if you wanted them for yourself. I did not want you to become a detective just because of me. I would rather you not attend the Academy and become exactly what you want to be. I believe this firmly, especially because of the danger of MUS, and more specifically Herr Zilch."

"In one of your letters, you said you didn't want me going to school just because of who you are—you're on the school board," said Rollie. "You also said something about who I will be. Does that have to do with our family lineage you mentioned a few months ago?"

Auntie Ei nodded. "Yes, but that discussion must keep for another day."

"Auntie, just tell me—"

Auntie Ei held up a wrinkled hand. "I will tell you when it is the right time. Will you trust me on this?"

Rollie nodded reluctantly.

"Good. Do remember to believe in yourself regardless of what other people think of you—even me. You will need to be sure of yourself if you are going to stand up against Herr Zilch. You know how he hates the Academy and me and now you."

"I know why he hates Sherlock Holmes—Holmes defeated Moriarty. Is that why he hates the Academy, or does it have something to do with your past history together? He was an associate of yours when you all worked at Scotland Yard together. Was he really a member of the Holmes Brigade just like you and the Yardslys?"

Auntie Ei pursed her lips. "Yes. The Holmes Brigade has been a classified division of the Yard for many years—long before Sherlock Academy. The Brigade was established to directly investigate, solve, and prevent MUS crime. When the Academy opened, the Yard established a student chapter of the Brigade to protect the school from MUS.

"The four of us—the Yardslys, Frederick Zilch, and myself—formed the first Holmes Brigade. Unknown to us, Zilch was working as a double agent for MUS. He betrayed not only the Brigade, but Scotland Yard as well. When we exposed him, he openly joined MUS and quickly became its leader."

"I thought the reason he hated you was because you got him fired."

"No, he got himself fired." Her voice grew soft and her eyes took on a faraway look as she remembered the past. "That was perhaps the darkest day of my life—the day Zilch betrayed us. He nearly killed us all, too . . . there was a fire . . . " She shook her head and her voice strengthened again. "You have no doubt seen his hands."

Rollie nodded. The past was making more sense. "Mr. Bartholomew Holmes told me you have to be invited to join the Holmes Brigade. Is there any chance of me getting invited?"

"That is not for me to decide. I am no longer an active Brigade member. After that incident in October with Watson's Case, I have decided to officially retire from Brigade and Yard duties. I shall continue to serve on the school board, but I am too old to be gallivanting after MUS." Auntie Ei closed her eyes. "I have a headache."

Rollie cast his eyes to the ground. "I'm sorry, Auntie."

"For what, may I ask? My headache?"

"For searching your room and for calling you an old woman."

"How absurd! I *am* an old woman, and you are a young man. However, I accept your apology in regards to your ransacking my room. I trust you will never give me cause to distrust you again."

"And I'm sorry for eavesdropping on you and Headmaster on Boxing Day," Rollie continued with a swallow. "I overheard you mention a will. Can you tell me more about that?"

Auntie Ei looked as if she was going to scold him, then softened and said, "Not today, Rollin. Anything else you have to apologize for?"

"Yes, Auntie. I doubted you and thought horrible things about you. I was angry. I'm sorry."

"I forgive you." She nodded, tucking a loose wisp of gray hair back into her bun. "I apologize for not giving you more credit as a detective and for having to keep secrets from you. All I ask for is your trust. Do remember I am always on your side."

Rollie turned to leave, then stopped. "I almost forgot. Zilch returned your underwear."

"Did he! Well, the day was not a complete failure then," she said with chuckle. "I do not suppose he returned Watson's Case."

"Yeah, he did. It's up in his study."

Auntie Ei brightened. "Thank heavens! Fetch it immediately."

Rollie left her in the library. Cecily and Eliot had joined Headmaster and Ms. Yardsly next door to investigate for clues regarding Wesley's abduction. He bundled up. His one sleeveless arm was a little cold beneath his sweater, but he did not notice. On the front porch, he paused, and collapsed on the steps. He would get the case for Auntie Ei, but first he needed a moment to catch his breath.

He was exhausted. While he was glad to have made amends with Auntie Ei and better understood her past, he was still confused. He wished she would tell him about his lineage—it would help him understand himself more.

He remembered Uncle Ky's words: *"Don't let people define you. If anything's going to define you, it should be your strong character and your moral convictions."*

Maybe Auntie Ei was right—maybe it was best he did not know about his lineage until he was absolutely sure of himself. He could not define himself out of obligation to others. Sherlock Holmes never did that. Holmes never cared what other people thought about him. As a result, he was a great detective.

As he pondered this, he spotted Euston Hood marching through the snow up the front walk. Euston carried Watson's Case with him and handed it to Rollie.

"I found this in Zilch's study. It was full of underwear," Euston said, his face reddening slightly. "Any idea—"

"It belongs to my Auntie Ei," Rollie said quickly. "All of it." With a grin, he told Euston how he had tricked Zilch with the Case.

Euston responded with a smile, which led to a chuckle. "Nice job. I'm sure that made Zilch's blood boil."

"Any luck finding Wesley, Mr. Hood?"

Euston's face clouded. "Not yet, but we will exhaust all resources to find him. We hope to gain information from the secretary. I better get back to helping Yardsly and Katherine." He turned to head back down the front walk to the street.

Suddenly, an idea lit up Rollie's face. "Mr. Hood! You're Herr Zilch's nephew, aren't you!"

Euston returned to the porch and joined Rollie on the front steps. "I was."

"That's your connection to MUS and Zilch. That's why Yardsly uses you as his spy. Zilch knew I knew you."

"That is all correct."

"We all think you are very brave, Mr. Hood, for turning on your uncle to help Sherlock Academy," Rollie said.

"Thank you. It was the hardest thing I have ever had to do." Euston stared off at the slushy street. "I no longer think of myself as Herr Zilch's nephew, or as the once-potential heir to MUS. Instead I am an ally to Sherlock Academy and all its participants. I am Herr Zilch's worst enemy."

"Auntie Ei wants to be sure I am choosing to be a detective for myself, especially because of the danger of Herr Zilch. I know I want to stop him no matter the cost."

"I think you proved that today." Euston locked eyes with him. "Mr. Wilson, I would like to officially invite you to join the Holmes Brigade."

Rollie's eyes widened. "Really? You have the authority to do that?"

Euston cracked an amused smile. "Yes, I do. As a member of the last Holmes Brigade, I have the privilege of selecting and advising the next Brigade. Today you proved you were willing to fight MUS no matter the cost. That's exactly who the Brigade needs."

"Who else will be in the Brigade with me? Aren't there always four members?"

"Yes, and the four members have specific jobs. There is always a master decoder, a master observer, a Baker Street Irregular, and an inspector. You'll make a perfect inspector. You are well rounded in all sleuth skills and exhibit extraordinary amounts of courage and leadership for your age."

Rollie beamed.

"I would like to invite Mr. Tildon as our decoder and Miss Brighton as our observer. You three work well together. Mr. Crisp has already been selected as the BSI."

"Rupert! We'll make a great team. Did you consider Wesley?"

Euston shook his head. "We need first-years for the new Brigade. This is Wesley's last year."

"So what's your job in your Brigade?"

Euston smiled again. "I'm the Baker Street Irregular. Sullivan Yardsly took me in when I betrayed my uncle and he disowned me. As an orphan, I've been working closely with Yardsly ever since to stop MUS. So will you accept my invitation?"

"Yes, Mr. Hood, yes! I can't wait to get to work against MUS."

Euston clapped Rollie on the back. "You've already been doing that, Rollie. This just makes it more official." He got up and headed next door.

Rollie watched him go but stayed put on the front step, growing colder as the brief daylight began to fade. He reflected on the past months since he had been attending Sherlock Academy. He remembered how he had exposed Zilch's agent Professor Enches and kept Zilch from gaining important personal information on the students and the school's alumni, many of whom had gone on to work with Scotland Yard. He remembered how he had intercepted Zilch's mole, Wesley, and kept Watson's manuscripts safe from MUS. He had done all this because he felt it was his duty to protect the school, not because anyone had pressured him to do it.

He wanted to be like Sherlock Holmes because he shared the great detective's love for mysteries and responsibility for upholding justice. Yes, Auntie Ei had introduced him to Holmes, but he himself had formed the attachment.

Rollie stood up. He set Watson's Case just inside the front door then headed next door. As he plowed through the snow toward Zilch's vacant house, he was met by Cecily and Eliot on their way back.

"Did Euston talk to you?" he asked them excitedly.

"Yes! He wants us to join the Holmes Brigade," Cecily squealed. "I'm so excited!"

"I need to think about it," said Eliot. "It's a dangerous position to be in."

Rollie patted his shoulder. "It is, Eliot. Oh, did Euston tell you he's Zilch's nephew?"

Cecily and Eliot gasped.

"*He's* the brave nephew?" Eliot shook his head in awe. "Crikey! And he thinks I'm brave enough to join his Holmes Brigade."

At that moment, Euston came through Zilch's garden gate and stopped next to the kids. "Listen, as the BSI of the last Brigade, I am the acting advisor for you. There are some formalities we need to fol-low for you to join the Holmes Brigade. There is an oath you'll take and training you'll need to start, but right now, Wesley's kidnapping is more pressing. So in the meantime, you can have these." Euston dug into his inner coat pocket and held out three leather wristbands etched with the Sign of the Four symbol.

Rollie and Cecily immediately grabbed them and snapped them around their wrists.

Eliot looked at the wristband, then up at Euston. "You're incredible, Mr. Hood, and you want me to join the Brigade. That means you must think I'm worthy. That's the way it works; brave people recog-nize other brave people." Eliot snatched the wrist-band and put it on.

"For once, you're making sense to me, Mr. Tildon."

Eliot grinned. "Would it be alright if I created a secret handshake for our Brigade? I'm thinking something that—"

"Don't get carried away." Euston placed a gloved hand on Eliot's shoulder. "I'm hopeful we'll uncover Zilch's Final Problem, I'm hopeful we'll find Wesley, and I'm hopeful we'll stop MUS once and for all."

Rollie grinned and held out his hand.

Solve more mysteries with Rollie and his friends in *Sherlock Academy* and *Sherlock Academy: Watson's Case*

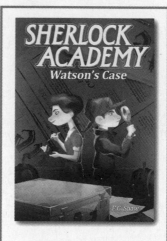

Join Rollie and Cecily as they investigate a strange burglary at Sherlock Academy and discover that appearances can be deceiving, the truth can be hurtful, and friends sometimes turn into foes.

In *Watson's Case*, you'll follow Rollie and Cecily as they work to catch a spy and decipher a secret map to thwart the evil Herr Zilch's plans!

"For everyone who's ever wanted to be Sherlock Holmes, this is your chance."

–Adam Glendon Sidwell, Bestselling Author of *Evertaster*

www.futurehousepublishing.com

Never miss a Future House release!

Sign up for the Future House Publishing email list:
www.futurehousepublishing.com/beta-readers-club

Connect with Future House Publishing

www.facebook.com/FutureHousePublishing

twitter.com/FutureHousePub

www.youtube.com/FutureHousePublishing

www.instagram.com/FutureHousePublishing

About the Author

F.C. Shaw started writing stories when she was eight years old. She loves children's stories, Sherlock Holmes, and mysteries, so had to write a book combining all three. She spends her afternoons writing for kids, and her nights dreaming of new stories. She lives with her husband and two sons in a home they have ambitiously dubbed *The Manor* in Santa Maria, California. When she's not plotting stories, she teaches visual arts in local schools and enjoys a good game of Scrabble.

Connect with the Author:
www.sherlockacademy.com
www.facebook.com/sherlockacademy

Want F.C. Shaw to come to your school?

F.C. Shaw's fun and interactive assembly encourages kids to explore their own imaginations. Using the great Sherlock Holmes and her own Sherlock Academy series as a base, she teaches kids how to write a mystery story by developing characters, creating a setting, placing clues, and devising a solution. F.C. Shaw's assembly is a perfect educational experience for your school.

For more information visit:
http://www.futurehousepublishing.com/
authors/fcshaw/

Or contact:
schools@futurehousepublishing.com